# A PLACE WITH A PAST

# A Place With A Past

Marlene Ratledge Buchanan

A Place with a Past

Copyright Marlene Ratledge Buchanan 2020

Marlene Ratledge Buchanan
MsRatWrites@gmail.com

Scribblers Press Inc
9741 SE 174th Place Road
Summerfield, FL 34491

US ISBN: 978-1-950308-30-9
Fiction: Romance, Fiction: Mystery

Library of Congress Control Number: 2020909087

Cover Picture by Marlene Ratledge Buchanan

Cover Designed by Black Water Arts – Katt Marshall

Initial Printing by: Trinity Press, Inc,
3190 Reps Miller Rd. Ste. 360, Norcross, GA 30071

## Disclaimer

Any similarity to anyone, living or dead, in this book is a coincidence. All characters are fictional.

## OOPS!

After numerous readings and re-writing of this material, I can promise you there will be mistakes. I tried. I really tried to get it right. The errors just proves I am human.

## In Gratitude

To all those students and friends who helped me through life. I appreciate and love you all.

Ms. Rat

Thank you, Randi Ward, for editing this book.

Special thanks and appreciation to Charles de Andrade of Scribblers Press. Without you, this would never have made it to print.

## Dedication

To Snell, the love of my life and our son, James, our special gift.

In Memory of my parents, James and Grace Ratledge.

## PROLOGUE

You never know what your day will bring. Things were going so well in my life; then my great aunt became ill. After her death, I found I had an extended family that had been dead for decades. Unfortunately, one was hateful and wanted to torment me.

# CHAPTER 1

In a daze, I walked out of the lawyer's office. I wondered what I would do with Great Aunt Belle and Great Uncle Charlie's farm. I had never thought about an inheritance. They had two children, but both had died many years ago. I guess I was the last of the family. Funny, I had never thought about being the end of the line.

When Aunt Belle needed care, I saw to it. I was with her at the hospital as much as possible. I held her hand for that last breath. She had a number of her church and community friends who were there as well. She had always given freely to the church and the special needs children's center. I guess I thought most of everything would go to them. It just never occurred to me she would leave all her worldly goods to me.

Ring-a-ding was my pet name for Aunt Belle. She was my maternal grandparent's sister-in-law but more like my grandmama's sister. They were best friends. She was a hoot. My mother was her favorite of all the nieces and nephews.

She had a joke for everything and loved to tell stories. Every time I would hear a funny tale, I would try to save it for her. I told her one time some of her jokes were getting a little dirty. She just laughed and said, "They're smoky, not dirty."

Ring-a-ding didn't cuss exactly. She knew all the words, but rarely did she set them free. I promise if you made her that mad, you deserved every word she gave you! Sweet Old Boy and Sweet Old Biddie were her favorite ugly sayings. You didn't want her to call you that either. It meant you had done something really bad that had irritated her gallbladder, as she would say.

Both of their children had died at young ages. Clarisse was about ten.

She had scarlet fever, and then pneumonia set in. I was trying to do the math, but I don't remember when she was born or when she died. I see the dates on the graves when I visit. I just don't remember them. I can't even tell you the date my parents died. It is just one of many quirks I have, I guess.

Belle's and Charlies' oldest child was Morton. He was named after Belle's side of the family. People used to use the mother's maiden name a lot for the son's first name. It doesn't seem to be done as much now.

Morton had a reputation as a daredevil and a fighter. I can remember Mama and Daddy talking about some of Morton's escapades. Even though he had been gone many years, he apparently was legendary—in an evil kind of way. Daddy said he was surprised someone hadn't killed him long before they did. Mama said he probably should have been lynched.

The story goes Morton was bad to drink. One night he got into a fight. The account I heard was Morton was messing around with this other man's wife. They got into a shouting match at the old Purvis Farm. Everyone knew old man Purvis had a liquor still. This was back in the 40's. Prohibition may have been over, but people still made their own white lightening. A lot of the people preferred it to the "store bought" kind.

A bunch of men had gathered to drink at the Purvis' barn. The husband and Morton were yah-yahing at each other. Morton pulled a gun. Morton always wore a side arm. The husband shoved Morton. There was a tiller in the barn with those disks that were used to cut up the soil. Morton fell back on the tines of the tiller. He had a bad head wound and had split his back open. He shot the man point blank while he was falling. Both men were taken to their homes. There weren't many hospitals. The doctor was called to the homes of the sick.

The husband lived in town and was closest to the doctor. The doctor went to the husband's house first. He treated him for the gunshot wound. The husband died the next day.

Later that night the doctor got to Morton. When he saw Morton, he told Ring-a-ding and Uncle Charlie if Morton lived, he'd never be the same. He had split his skull open. Morton lived for four more days.

I don't believe Aunt Belle and Uncle Charlie ever really got over Morton's death. It was rare Morton was mentioned. Maybe they wanted to forget him and all the pain he caused. Maybe they just silently mourned him. Morton's room was never used.

Ring-a-ding and Uncle Charlie did talk about Clarisse. She was their baby girl, and they adored her. Clarisse's cheerful room was kept open. Aunt Belle kept her treadle sewing machine and fabrics in Clarisse's room. Morton's room was closed off. To my memory I had never been in that room. I don't remember ever seeing the door open.

# CHAPTER 2

The old house was a wood frame with huge front and back porches. When the old kitchen in the back yard burned down, they converted one of the back rooms into the new kitchen. Water was hauled to the house in a bucket. I remember the bucket sitting on the old wood burning stove. It had a tin ladle in it. If you wanted a drink of water, you got it from the bucket. Everyone used the same ladle. It was a great day when an electric pump was installed to run water to the kitchen.

Some time, years later, Uncle Charlie decided they needed an indoor bathroom and a water heater. That was going to be a big change in their lives. Belle had an old wringer washing machine sitting on the back porch. She still boiled her towels and sheets in the old kettle in the back yard. Now she would be able to machine wash clothes in hot water.

Charlie and a couple of the farm hands put up a wall on one end of the back porch. They framed in a bathroom. I think Ring-a-ding was prouder of the indoor toilet than she was of the hot water.

Everyone that came to the house had to see the bathroom. It was pink and her pride and joy. Uncle Charlie drew the line at having a pink toilet, but he did paint the room her favorite color. It had pink flowered linoleum on the floor. I don't think any insulation was put under the house. It was always cold in there. My daddy put in an electric wall heater which helped a lot. The floor never was warm though.

People saved old clothes for fabric scraps to make rugs or quilts. Aunt Belle loved to quilt. She crocheted and created braided rugs, too. They were placed on the kitchen and bathroom floors. Each side of the bed had one of her rugs. They gave a little protection from the cold. In the winter your feet still felt as if they would freeze to the floor.

A refrigerator and a gas stove were eventually installed. A big truck would deliver propane gas every six months or so. Aunt Belle had left the huge wood burning cook stove in the kitchen. It was a Home Comfort cast iron beast. It kept the kitchen warm in the winter and hot as all get out in the summer.

After the modernization of the kitchen, Aunt Belle used the old stove to store pots and pans in the oven. The burner top was covered with her African violets. I believe she had one in every color. She rooted philodendron in water. The top of the stove always had one or two vases with the vines cascading almost to the floor.

# CHAPTER 3

I sat in the car in front of the old house, just remembering odd things. I had my keys. I had been in several times to feed the critters and to take care of odds and ends. I usually ran in and out. The last time I spent any time in the house was to get Ring-a-ding's funeral dress, a royal blue and cream-colored suit, which she had worn to Uncle Charlie's funeral. When we left the cemetery that day, we were walking hand in hand back to the car. "Baby, when my time comes, I want to be buried in this same dress. It was Charlie's favorite and mine, too."

I told her that suit would have disintegrated by the time she needed it for her funeral. She laughed and asked me if I knew why they put pennies on dead people's eyes. I knew it was one of her bad jokes. "No, why, Ring-a-ding?"

"Cause even the devil wouldn't give two cents for them. They have to pay their way in." That was typical of her jokes. She would laugh and clap her hands. I would get a case of the giggles just watching her being entertained by her own humor. She was funnier telling the stories than the stories were funny.

The key ring from the lawyer was larger than the set I had. I guess his had all the out- buildings. One I did recognize. It went to the new barn. The new barn was probably a good fifty years old, but it was still called the new barn. The older barn was called the crib. The crib was made of stacked wooden poles. Most people identified them as "pole barns." I don't know why this was the crib. It had always been called that. Maybe, it stored corn at one time and was the "corn crib." I have no idea. There was an old wagon sitting on the lean-to side of the crib. That wagon has sat there for as long as I could remember. I bet there was thirty pounds of chicken droppings on it.

I finally got out of the car. I was tired. It had been a long day and an emotional one, too. I had to wait on the lawyer to get back to his office. When he finally arrived, having forgotten our appointment, I was fit to be tied. He gave me the will and the keys and told me I was the sole heir. I was with him perhaps all of fifteen minutes.

I stopped in town at one of the fast food places to pick up something to eat. As soon as I could, I would take a shower in Ring-a-ding's prized pink bathroom. Then I was going to bed. The back bedroom next to the kitchen was the room I always slept in. It had two old wrought iron beds in it. When Uncle Charlie got too feeble for the stairs, they moved to the back room. Ring-a-ding slept in the bed closest to the bathroom. I slept in the other bed that had been Uncle Charlie's.

In the morning I would need to take care of some of her business affairs. I would feed the chickens and try to find them a home. I wish I could take the guinea hen back to my house. She makes the neatest racket when she talks. Her name is Guinea Girl. She followed Ring-a-ding around like a puppy. It wasn't uncommon to find Aunt Belle and Guinea Girl sitting on the back porch together. Belle would be rocking, and Guinea Girl would be nesting in her wooden box.

Two cats Ramona and Randolph had lived with Aunt Belle. She was such a softie about animals, and animals just loved her. Ramona and Randolph were supposed to be more barn cats than house cats. Ring-a-ding brought them in every morning to eat breakfast and spend some time with her. Truth be known, I suspect those cats spent their nights in the house, too. She combed them every day. I guess it was a ritual with which I had best get familiar.

That night I fell into my bed. I believe I was asleep almost as soon as my head hit the pillow. During the night I woke up to hear the old house sighing. I thought to myself, "I miss her, too."

# CHAPTER 4

The next morning, I fed the chickens. Guinea Girl came up to me. We had a conversation while she ate her scratch feed. Ramona and Randolph came right on into the house. Randolph went to Aunt Belle's bed. He jumped up and sniffed around. He turned and looked at me as if he were saying "Where's Mama?" I told the two of them she wasn't coming home anymore. I tried to explain to them we'd be living together at my house in town. Ramona looked up at me and flipped her tail. She lay down next to Randolph on the bed and watched me.

All day I dealt with the affairs of the deceased. I must have made a dozen phone calls. I had to go to the grocery store and the bank. I left the cats on Ring-a-ding's bed while I got myself ready to go to town.

I explained my missions for the day. I would be home in a couple of hours. Randolph yawned as if it were all just too much for him. Ramona didn't even open an eye.

I took care of what I could. The old Piggly Wiggly was some other name now, but folks still called it The Piggly Wiggly. The black and white tile floor had never been changed.

It took much longer for me get the few things the cats and I needed. Ring-a-ding had been a force in the community. She was a well-respected and well-thought-of force. I was stopped repeatedly by different people offering sympathy and assistance. That was the thing about this little town. Everyone knew your business. If you needed help, they were there for you. Do something you shouldn't, and you were the talk of the town. "Frowned on" was how Ring-a-ding described someone who had behaved badly. "The whole town frowned on him."

After I unloaded the groceries, I came out to sit on the back porch. The two cats joined me. Ramona jumped in my lap. I brushed her black and white fur until it glistened. When she got down, Randolph, a big grey tabby, came to me. We went through all the combing and primping for him.

# CHAPTER 5

I had to make decisions about what I was going to do. When I returned from college, I had rented a house in town less than a mile from the high school in which I taught. Now I had this place. It was about nine miles further out of town, but it would be rent free. Of course, there would be the taxes and other expenses. This was an old house. It had been built long before Aunt Belle and Uncle Charlie married. They were together 67 years when Uncle Charlie died. I should make a list of the pros and cons of keeping it. I would need someone to assess the condition and to determine if anything needed to be done. This had to be completed before I decided to sell or to stay.

Of course, if I kept the house, Guinea Girl could wake me up every morning.

Even though it was summer, it had been cloudy all day. It seemed as if night was coming on early. I asked the cats to join me for dinner. As we ate, I decided I would go on to bed. Visiting with so many people at the grocery store had been very emotional and tiring.

Tomorrow I would ask Mr. Herman if he could help me find someone to determine the condition of the house. He and his wife were neighbors, living about a mile up the road toward town. They had helped Aunt Belle a lot. Ring-a-ding had taught Miss Hazel to play the pump organ and the piano.

I had no idea of what might be in Uncle Charlie's desk. I needed to go through it next, I supposed. I felt very overwhelmed thinking of all the things that had to be done. I was still terribly emotional about losing Aunt Belle. She died on the last day of school. I was tired from work—tired from grieving.

While she was in the hospital, I went to Belle's place every day to check on things. She had a young man who came by twice a day. He let the chickens out and fed them every morning. He came by every night to put them up.

I dropped in to check on her cats daily. If I had taken them home with me, it would have been easier for me. Belle was convinced they needed to be at her place. It wasn't worth arguing over. If I had been in my right mind, I would have taken the cats to my house and not told her. I was that tired and upset I never thought of that simple solution.

That night I awoke to that same sighing sound. Ramona had gone to bed with me, and Randolph had joined us during the night. He stood up and bushed his tail as if something was after him.

That sigh. A groan? No, I was just listening to the sounds of an old house. I had never slept alone in this house. I remembered the old chimney used to whistle when the wind was bad. That would scare the pee-turkey out of me. Finally, she had that fixed. It just needed the guard on the chimney reset. It had been a simple solution.

# CHAPTER 6

I didn't sleep well that night. Maybe it was the sounds of the house. I wasn't used to sleeping with cats, either. Those little fur babies thought they needed to be with me. I guess I wanted them there. I certainly didn't shoo them off the bed.

I would drift off to sleep only to awake from a weird dream. I swear someone talked to me all night long with soft little whispers and deep sighs.

The next morning while I was making coffee, I listened to Guinea Girl talking from the old oak tree in the back yard. I decided to make a list of all the things that popped into my mind. Pros and cons about remaining in the old house would be one sheet. What repairs would be needed to be done on another. I would use a third sheet for odd thoughts and reminders, like phone calls. Gosh, that sounded easy. Yikes, I knew the lists were going to be long and not at all easy.

About eight years ago, Ring-a-ding sold all the timber off the farm. I forgot how many years ago those old fields had been planted with pines. They were huge trees. Once cleared, she had that land replanted by the state forestry department. These pines would be ready to harvest probably in fifteen or so years, I thought.

It had been a tidy sum of money. She had always wanted a "tin roof" instead of the asphalt shingles. "I want a red roof and a scarlet front door." She had said. "I want people to know that I am here and still mean as a STRI-pped snake!" I can remember her curving her fingers like snake fangs while striking and hissing at me. She got tickled then. I thought I would pass out from laughing.

Of course, she wasn't mean as a snake, and people did know her. She and Uncle Charlie had been generous to those who worked on the farm. They raised cattle, hogs, farmed cotton, and sugarcane originally. They did turpentine gathering from all those pines, too. If people in town fell on hard times, either one or both would show up at the house with food and a helping hand. They lived the Golden rule. They expected nothing in return.

After Uncle Charlie's death, friends showed up whenever she needed something. She didn't have to ask. I remember a bad storm came through one night. An enormous limb from the old pecan tree fell on the hen house. It was a small frame structure. No chickens were harmed in the storm. That was important. All her chickens, each had a name, were just fine.

The morning after, two different families came by to check on her. Her phone was out. During the day, more people stopped in. All of them were carrying food. They just cared about her. By that evening, the hens had a deluxe apartment, and Ring-a-ding had a cell phone.

I can't tell you how long I had begged her to have a cell phone and one of those emergency button necklaces. I kept telling her she could fall and would need help. No one would know until someone stopped in, or I called after work. Nope, it took putting the chickens in danger to get her a cell phone. Silly ol' doll.

# CHAPTER 7

The cats and I decided to look through the four rooms upstairs. I couldn't remember when I had spent time in any of the rooms except Belle's. The last time was to get Uncle Charlie's favorite dress for her to wear to her own funeral. "I'll be seeing my ol' boy soon. I can hardly wait." She told me that last day in the hospital. She met Uncle Charlie a few hours later.

Randolph and Ramona had obviously visited Belle's and Charlie's room many times. There were two cat-sized furry depressions on the white chenille spread. Randolph roamed about the room, checking out the corners. Ramona landed softly on top of the bed and began to circle her spot. I am pretty sure she was smiling. I could hear her purrs from across the room.

I made a note on the pad the stair rail needed to be tightened. As I looked around the room, I noticed the little "rat's nest." Ladies would save the hair that collected on their brush after grooming. Belle's was a milk glass hobnail one. The little hole in the top showed a few hairs were still inside. Belle had cut her long hair years ago. The doctor told her it was the weight of all her hair that was causing a lot of her headaches. I do remember brushing that long hair. When she sat in the rocker, it almost touched the floor. "Gather that loose hair. I may need my rat to poof up my hair one day."

Mama would tell her she wasn't a Gibson Girl anymore and didn't need her rat. Belle would shimmy a little and laugh, "Honey, you never know. I still have my corsets. I could get all dolled up and sashay through in town. I could still knock 'em dead." Daddy told her he didn't think he had the strength to tighten those corsets. She smacked him on the fanny. Come to think of it, I think Aunt Belle might have had a thing for Daddy's fanny. She would pop him on it every chance she got. That dirty old Ring-a-ding.

Randolph and I went through the chifforobe. The clothes there were really old. She wore her house dresses with an apron pinned to them every day. She dressed up for Church on Sunday morning. All her current wardrobe was kept in the chifforobes downstairs.

I found Uncle Charlie's black beaver dress hat in an octagon-shaped hat box on the top of the old wardrobe. He was always neat as a pin and debonairly dressed. Aunt Belle saw to that. He still had two good suits hanging in the chifforobe—a heavy black wool and a lighter weight black one. They were both in a dry cleaner bag. He was buried in gray suit with a blue tie. I remember looking at him and thinking how beautiful the suit was with his white hair.

I looked at Randolph, "If we stay up here any longer, we are turning on the air conditioning." It was already hot, and it hadn't hit noon yet. Belle had installed central heat and air when she did all the "lumber money fixing-up."

She had also had her pink bathroom redone. It was still pink but better insulated and with new fixtures. Daddy had convinced her to take out the bathtub and put in a walk-in shower. She was having trouble stepping into the tub. She fell one time. Mama and Daddy had stopped by, thank goodness. They had just come in the kitchen door about the time she hit the floor.

"Nekkid as the day I was born. Laying in the floor with one foot up in the air. Nothing to cover me. Nekkid as a jay bird. Your mama called an ambulance. When they got there, your daddy had already looked me over and picked up my poor ol' nekkid self. He just picked me up in his arms and carried me to the bed. Me, nekkid."

The way Daddy convinced her to replace the bathtub with a shower was to tell her, "Belle, I've seen you naked once. I will remember that image for the rest of my life. Do you want someone else to find you naked in the floor? Get a shower you can walk into."

"None, but Charlie and the good Lord have ever seen me nekkid. Now your daddy has. Get me one of them Stewart boys out here." The Stewart Family owned the Home Depot store. It was never Home Depot. It was always the "Stewart Boys' place."

Now you know as well as I do if the Stewart Boys owned the business, they were not the ones to come out and take care of the actually planning and installation. Danny Stewart showed up the next day though. Belle was in her bed. She was sore from her fall but still sassy—and still angry about being found "nekkid."

After inquiring about Danny's entire family and sharing a story or two about his mama, Ring-a-ding told him what she wanted. Daddy sat beside her and nodded his head when she looked at him. Danny said, "I'll be back tomorrow, Miss Belle."

"Tell your mama hey for me. Bring her to see me sometime when she can get out. Hug Terri and all the little ones. Tell Evan I said to come see me." The ritual of a southern goodbye.

# CHAPTER 8

Daddy and Danny sat out on the back porch and discussed what really needed to be done in the old bathroom. The next day, Danny and his brother Evan came out to the house. Miss Lucille was with them. She was really crippled with arthritis, but this must have been one of her better days. Evan helped her up the front steps.

Belle and Miss Lucille had the best time that day. Evan, Danny, Daddy, and Mama visited. Within minutes after the Stewart boys got there a truck showed up. Three men started tearing out the old bathtub. By nine that night, Aunt Belle had a brand new bathroom. It still needed painting, but everything was done from floor to ceiling.

Mama had cooked dinner, and everyone came to the table, including the men working on the bathroom. There was enough food for five more. Aunt Belle knew all the men working in her house. They had grown up here. She and Charlie went to school with most of their grandparents.

One of the men's father had worked for was Uncle Charlie. Mr. John was hurt when he turned over the tractor while tilling for spring planting. He was a widower. His oldest daughter and her family lived with him in the old home place.

As long as Mr. John lived, Uncle Charlie took him his paycheck every Friday. I guess that was a pension of sorts. Mr. John didn't walk again. He used to whittle. I still have the little animals he carved. Uncle Charlie would always buy me one of Mr. John's "treasures." I remember his grandkids had a Noah's Ark that he had carved. The boat was made of pine and had a shingled roof made from the scaly clusters of pine-cone seeds. Two of every animal you could think of were with it. Mr. John has been gone a long time. I would love to see Noah's Ark again. It should be in a folk-art museum.

# CHAPTER 9

I went into Clarisse's room where Aunt Belle stored her fabrics and treadle sewing machine. Clarisse had a little porcelain headed doll. The body was of pink and blue satin. She wasn't wearing any clothes, just that fabric body. Someone had hung a little gold cross around the doll's neck. The cross was probably Clarisse's. The bed was covered with a pale pink chenille spread. Folded at the foot was a pink, white, and yellow quilt. The pattern was butterflies. I imagine the mattress was one of those old feather stuffed ones. That was the kind downstairs on Belle's and Charlie's beds.

Ramona joined Randolph in the exploration of Clarisse's room. She found a spider. Ramona was in hog heaven. She tormented that poor thing. I don't think she killed it. I think it just gave up the ghost on its own. I added "Call exterminator" to my to-do list.

The drawers all had Belle's material folded neatly in them. In the chifforobe she had stacked completed quilts. I couldn't imagine how long ago those were made. In one of the other rooms was the old quilting frame. It took up a good bit of space. There were two old farm tables sitting together where Aunt Belle laid out her materials to cut and baste. Those tables made a good six-foot square workspace. This would make a good office. I could use both of those tables.

I could use one as a desk for the computer. The other would be great to lay out my writing projects and school papers. I wonder if I could turn one of the chifforobes into storage for books and supplies. If the big quilting frame were gone, I could put one table on the side wall and the other under the window. There would be a lot of natural light.

If I stayed. Where did that come from? I was kind of getting a little ahead of myself.

This was another issue with an old house. No closets. The tax accessor counted a closet as a room. Each room had a tax on it. People didn't build closets. They used free standing pieces of furniture as armoires. There was at least one in each of the rooms. I wondered if Morton or Clarisse's rooms could be divided to make closets and an upstairs bathroom. When I moved in, I would need an upstairs bathroom.

There was that thought again.

# CHAPTER 10

The cats and I returned downstairs. I had added a few things to my list. If I kept her house, would I move into Belle's and Charlie's room upstairs? Four up and four down was the layout. One thing was sure; I wouldn't need any furniture. I was in a museum of antiques-dust and goosal-feather protected antiques.

WHEN I moved in. Now, here was an interesting change in my thought patterns. Before it had been IF, now it was when. Am I really going to move into Belle's place? I have plenty of time to decide about where I would live. My place in town was so much more convenient. It was a much more modern, too.

I really needed to think this through. Sentimentality was certainly playing a part in the decision-making process. I must remove all the sentimental and emotional aspects from the decision-making activity. I had to think about this more rationally. Where did I put that pros and cons list?

I made a peanut butter and blackberry jelly sandwich and reheated the morning's coffee. The cats were nibbling at their crunchies. The pros and cons pad lay on the table.

| Pro | Con |
|---|---|
| No rent | Taxes, more than rent |
| Guinea Girl and the cats | Second floor bathroom needed |
| More space | No closets |
| | House upkeep |
| | Yard upkeep |
| | Greater distance to work |
| | No garage |
| | Cold floors |
| | Pepto-Bismol Kitchen |
| | Two-story house |
| | PINK bathroom |

So far, the cons were winning. I was also thinking about money. I had not made it to the bank yesterday. I should go soon. I needed to know the financial standing and go through all her accounts. I had enough money in our joint account to continue to pay the bills. Eventually I would have to move money from somewhere. Ring-a-ding never seemed to worry about money. She wasn't a spend thrift until she got the lumber money. That scarlet door and roof just delighted her. After she re-modeled, I don't think she bought anything else.

I wrote a note on the to-do list to call the man who did her accounts. I thought the timber would keep this listed as agricultural land for tax purposes, but I wasn't sure. I had not found her tax folders for this year in the desk, either.

# CHAPTER 11

About two years ago she asked if I would start paying her bills. She had added me to her checking account. Her bills were mostly utility accounts and chicken feed.

Mr. Melvin lived about half a mile from her. Mr. Melvin, his wife, Myrtle, and my mother had grown up together. Their grand boy Tony helped with the yards and errands. Belle wanted the yards swept as they did a hundred years ago. She told me it was to keep the grass away, so you didn't have to tend to it, and if a snake came up, you'd see it. "I can't stand a snake!" she'd say.

Tony's was really the only regular payment outside of utilities she had. She paid him $50.00 a week to keep the yards swept. Occasionally, she would ask him to take care of some odds and ends for her. Some days he would have a good bit to do. Other days he would just sweep the yards and come in to visit. Sweeping the yards was always one of his tasks.

He came every Wednesday, more often if she needed him. He was Belle's only employee. Tony did just about everything for her. He did all the little odd jobs needed and kept her company. I suspected she gave Tony an extra $20 often. She would remind me to bring her five $20 bills from the bank each month.

Tony picked up the chicken feed. He set it up in the old building by the hen house. He ripped the bag open and rolled the bag top so Ring-a-ding could get out the scratch to feed the birds. When she could no longer go out and do it herself, Tony began coming by every afternoon. He would put her in the wheelchair and roll her outside. He gathered feed in a bowl so she could scatter it. The chickens came to her. She would "visit with the girls." She and Tony would spend time out in the yard. He'd roll her around so she could look at her flowers. Guinea Girl would follow them around like a dog. It was sight to see.

Aunt Belle adored Tony. I know for a fact last Christmas she bought him a new suit of clothes. As teenagers are prone to do, Tony had a growth spurt. Suddenly nothing was long enough. I took her and Tony to the Gentry Shop in town. Tony kept trying to pick out something cheap. "NO, Boy. I want you to have a decent suit of clothes. You'll need a good suit to be my pall bearer, and you got other things you can use that suit for. You dress like a man who is successful-not a want-to-be, but someone who-is-a-success."

Tony left with a navy suit, two pair of dress pants, one khaki and one grey, four dress shirts and four ties. She fitted him in socks and a pair of black wingtip shoes. While Tony was trying on things, she told the salesman to put him ten pair of 'new drawers and t-shirts' in the bag, and don't you say anything about that underwear to that boy. He'd die of embarrassment."

Tony always came in the house. He would visit for a few minutes with Aunt Belle. Most of the time he'd bring her something sweet. Sometimes his mama would send dinner. About once a month his grandparents would come to visit with him. Myrtle was well known for her cakes. She always brought a Lady Baltimore cake with nuts and cherries. Belle would put the coffee on. You could hear them laughing all the way to the new barn. Belle had a loud, joyous laugh.

Speak of the devil, the phone rang. Tony was on the line. "Miss Patricia, do you need me for anything? Tomorrow is the day I am supposed to come to sweep the yards. Do you want me to still do that?"

I assured Tony his job was secure and to come on. I also asked him if he would help me look through the yards and the barns. I didn't know what was out there, but I really didn't want to wander around in the back lots alone.

# CHAPTER 12

Tony came the next morning. He poured himself a cup of coffee. I was fixing my breakfast, so I doubled the eggs, grits and bacon. He told me he had eaten breakfast at home. Well, of course, he had already eaten. Everyone eats a good breakfast in this part of the country, but I fed him anyway. He ate it all along with several pieces of toast with jelly. I am not sure you can fill up a teenage boy. Mama used to say all teenagers had a hollow leg. "You just can't fill them up. As soon as you get one leg full, the other is empty."

He told me about school. In his upcoming senior year, he wanted to take an auto-mechanics class at the vocational high school. He planned to attend the diesel mechanics program at the technical college when he graduated next June.

Tony was like his daddy. He never met a piece of machinery he didn't like. His daddy could fix anything. I suspected Tony could, too.

We wandered about the back lots. "Miss Patty, are you going to move in here?"

I told him I just didn't know what I wanted to do. I was torn between going back to my little house in town and moving into Belle's place. We talked on about things. He suggested I ask his daddy about the condition of the old house and farm. He said his daddy was the electrician who had rewired the house for Aunt Belle during the remodel. He knew the old house pretty well.

We found an old saddle in the loft of the crib. The leather was dry rotted. There was a tricycle and an old gun stock. There must have been two dozen dusty Mason jars. The cardboard box holding them had pretty well disintegrated. Not anything of value. On the bottom floor were old feed sacks, more deteriorated cardboard boxes with nasty Mason jars, and some yard tools. We left everything and wandered down to the new barn.

Tony got a ladder. The original one was pretty rickety. He helped me up into the loft. We found two old moldering bales of hay. Tony pushed them both out the loft door into the lot yard. Within minutes the chickens were tearing them apart. I was sure there were plenty of tasty bugs.

Other than some old rope and a couple of wooden baskets the top floor was empty. I could remember climbing up here to shuck corn kernels off so the chickens, geese, and turkeys would come eat. What was that old tom turkey's name? He was huge and mean as a wild hog. I was scared of him.

Downstairs we found a treasure trove of old wooden tool and feed boxes painted that haint blue color. That is the same color painted on the porch ceilings to ward off ghosts and mean spirits. There was an ammo box with some shotgun shells. I would be afraid to fire one. I told Tony I would call the sheriff and ask if they would pick them up and destroy them.

We found a very large trunk that probably belonged to Aunt Belle's or Uncle Charlie's ancestors. It had a pair of overalls and brogan shoes-well worn. There was a print dress with violets on it. The collar had tatting on it. I remembered that dress from when I was little. I didn't pull everything out, but I could see a bunch of embroidery patterns, some other clothes, shoes and books.

About that time, I heard a yelp. I must have jumped three feet because when I landed, I was facing Tony. He was laughing. "Miss Patricia, there is a Warf rat in this old feed bin. You want me to go to the truck and get my shotgun and kill him?"

I suggested we leave him in peace and go back to the house. I really didn't want a dead rat stinking up the barn. If we saw him out in the yards, then we could kill him. That blood inside the barn would just invite more critters. Tony told me that rat was probably bigger than Randolph. Randolph at 18 pounds was not a tiny little cat.

# CHAPTER 13

Aunt Belle had left an envelope for Tony with me. While she was still strong and getting about, she told me Tony was the greatest help she had. Often, he would stop on the way home from school to check on her. She wanted him to have his education completely paid for. She wanted him to have the new blue truck. Tony and his daddy were working on an old '49 Ford truck that had belonged to his granddaddy, Mr. Melvin.

They had that old truck running, but it wasn't reliable. Ring-a-ding didn't like the idea of Tony not having a good car. While she was alive, she tried to buy him a truck. He absolutely refused so she bought a new truck for her farm and gave him a set of keys. He was welcome to use it anytime and for anything.

When the old Ford was not being cooperative, he'd ask if he could borrow "the blue truck." She told him a thousand times he didn't need to ask. He always did though.

He put running boards on the blue truck, so Aunt Belle could get into the cab. Tony would take Ring-a-ding out for a ride sometimes. She loved it. Almost every time they went out, they stopped at the Dairy Queen. Her favorite ice cream was Peanut Buster Parfaits with extra hot fudge.

Once, Tony brought her to the high school on a teacher's workday, so she could see my classroom. Most of the people in the school knew her. She had a grand old time visiting with everyone.

Ring-a-ding and I mostly went places in my car. She could get in and out of a vehicle easily until this last year. We went to the grocery store every Tuesday afternoon—whether she needed anything or not. It was her time to see and be seen. She would dress up almost as much as she did to go to church.

In that envelope was the title to the blue truck. She included a note explaining he was to go on to school. There was money set up to pay for his education.

I gave him the envelope. As he read the letter, he cried. "She was the kindest person in the world to me and my family. I can't take this. She did so much for us."

"Tony, you will take the truck. We will get it signed over into your name. You will also go on to school, and let Aunt Belle pay for it. She loved you as if you were her own grandson. If you don't do this, she will haunt you and me both. You know it is true!"

He laughed. "Yes, Ma'am. I know. She came to me in a dream the other night and told me to clean up the chicken house. She hasn't gone anywhere, has she? She's still in the house. You know I took her to the cemetery the first week of every month, sometimes more often. Mama did it before I did. She would walk around and check on everyone, not just y'all's plot."

I knew. I, too, took her at least once a month to check on things. Every month she would change the flowers on Uncle Charlie's, her children's, and my parent's graves. She had been planting iris along the edges inside the coping. It was beautiful when they bloomed.

# CHAPTER 14

Aunt Belle loved jewelry, especially broaches. She had a broach in every color for every outfit. Uncle Charlie had bought a wooden toolbox which had lots of shallow drawers. The drawers were only three inches deep. He had planned to use it for screw drivers and those kinds of small tools.

She saw that blond oak toolbox on the back of the truck and zeroed in on it. Before Charlie knew what had happened, it was upstairs in their bedroom. She must have spent two days sorting and placing her jewelry in those little drawers. Each drawer held a different color.

One day I saw a deep purple scarf with pink and white peonies printed on it. It just looked like Ring-a-ding. I bought it and wrapped it up as a little treat. We were always giving each other stuff we didn't need. It was "just a little treat."

After that, she couldn't get enough scarves. There was an old humpback trunk upstairs. I didn't really know what all was in it, probably papers and books. One day she called me at work. She asked me to bring her a couple of boxes of quart sized zip-lock bags. "I want one of those plastic tubs that has a lid on it. Not a really big one, but big enough for what I need." Then she hung up. I had no idea what size bin she needed. I'd just guess.

I showed up with her requests after work. "Ring-a-ding. It's me. Where are you?"

"Up here. I am in a hell of a mess. Did you bring me a box and those bags? I need you and them up here."

When I got to the top of the steps, I found her sitting in the floor surrounded by stacks of musty papers. "What in the world are you into now?"

"Baby, I got down here and I can't get up. I have sat on this floor too long. Every joint in my body has stiffened up."

Her cell phone was in her apron pocket. Her emergency button was safety pinned to the bib of her apron. She hadn't called for help. Lord have mercy. What was I going to do with her?

I got her up. She walked around the room alternating between squatting, standing up and shaking her legs. "Good. I am loose as a goose." She just amazed me. "I need to go to the bathroom, and I want a cup of coffee." She told me many times "coffee is my most important meal of the day." The pot was always ready.

When we went back upstairs, I asked her to tell me what she needed done. "I want all these papers put in that plastic tub. Can you do that for me?"

I asked what the papers were. She just grunted and said "Old crap. I'll keep it, but I don't think any of it is any good. There is an old deed to the back pasture in there. You might put that somewhere safe and Clarisse's little Bible."

She left the room a few minutes later with the small Bible. She was empty handed when she came back.

I put the deed and few other items she had laid to one side on the little table in front of the window. The rest I straightened and placed in the box. There were some old letters from people I didn't know. She had found a stack of handkerchiefs and a few old table runners. Belle said her mama had used those handkerchiefs to teach her and her sister how to embroider.

"They are not the prettiest work we ever did, except for Mama's, but I think I am going to make a little quilt out of them. I might add a few more of Mama's that I have. I think it would be a sweet little baby quilt or maybe a lap throw. I might crochet a border. I have some fine gage variegated purple crochet thread. Wouldn't that be pretty? Who knows, maybe you'll give me a great-great something or other."

I thought at the rate I was going, that won't happen. I had been dating the local pharmacist for about a year now. William had moved here for his job. He was originally from a little town about a hundred miles away. We had never really talked seriously about marriage.

Ring-a-ding liked William a lot. He often brought her medicine on his way home from work. He always stayed a while "just to visit." He lived about two miles further down this road. William was a caring man. He stood beside me through all the funeral and graveside preparations and services. He gave me strength during those hard times.

William called every night about 9:15. That was the time he usually got home when he worked late. We'd share a little of our day with each other. He was an important part of my life. Husband? He'd make a good one. But for me?

She had a bundle of scarves. They had hung on the back of her bedroom door. She would fuss because they would catch in the door jamb every time she closed it. She had the bright idea to use the old humpback trunk for her scarves.

While I had been taking care of the papers, she had cleaned the inside of that trunk. Sometime back I had given her a little hand-held vacuum cleaner. She would chase the old tomcat that lived here with it. He would stalk the vacuum cleaner. When she would turn it on, he would jump up and run around in circles. As soon as she turned it off, Thomas would come back for more.

We started folding her scarves and putting them in the zip-lock bags. "Lay them out by color now. I want to find the color I need without having to paw through everything."

It took us about an hour, but the humpback trunk was perfect for what she wanted. In the tray, she laid all her silk flower pins she had made. She changed the flowers on her hats to match her outfits.

On Sunday's she would wear a scarf that matched the outfit. It would be pinned to her bosom with a matching broach. Even her flat shoes would match her dress. She was styling.

# CHAPTER 15

I called the church ladies to offer them Belle's quilting fabrics. She had a lot of cloth. There was enough backing and padding for several more quilts as well. The church ladies were thrilled. Most of them had quilted with Belle at one time or another. Several of their guild quilts had won awards at the fair.

The church ladies had created a sewing guild, The Queenagers, years ago. They also did crochet work. Some days it looked like an afghan factory in the church's gathering room. The pieces were given to people who could use them. The local assisted living home had a huge stack of the Afghans available when someone needed a little extra cover. The Queenagers made matching crocheted baby caps, socks and blankets. Each newborn was given a set when they left the hospital.

One of my former students came with her mother and the others to take the fabric. This was another good excuse for them all to visit. I had iced tea and chocolate chip cookies ready on the back porch when they arrived.

Dana was telling me that she was quilting now. She was learning on a small frame. Dana and two of her friends had an on-line arts and crafts business. They made baby quilts, pillows, toys and other things from fabric. The business was doing quite well. She showed me some pictures on her phone. She had made some teddy bears out of children's clothes for people. I asked if she could make me a bear from one of Belle's old dresses and Uncle Charlie's overalls. She had never done something quite like that, but she was as excited as I was as we discussed the project.

I gave her Aunt Belle's big quilting frame. There was a smaller one in the upstairs sewing room. I kept it for now. I would never do a big quilt.

I didn't enjoy that. I did do embroidery work. I had learned from Mama, Grandmama, and Aunt Belle. I was not very accomplished. I'd rather read a book if I had free time.

# CHAPTER 16

The cats and I went upstairs to look at Clarisse's bedroom and the old sewing room. They were now very empty of everything but the furniture. It seemed odd not to have that clutter. Randolph sat on top on the treadle sewing machine. Aunt Belle used that manual Singer sometimes to turn a hem. She had a big White & Co. sewing machine, a cabinet model. She said Uncle Charlie got it for her just after the end of World War II. She loved her old Singer more.

I had decisions to make. Most of Belle's clothing would not be good for anyone. The things upstairs had not been worn for years. I thought about giving it all to Dana for fabric. Some of the pieces were lovely with that old tatted lace. Some were embroidered. Dana could create some beautiful items from it all. I would talk to her and her friends about it. I was thinking I'd use that violet print dress and Uncle Charlie's overalls for my teddy bear.

There was Clarisse's baby dress in one the chifforobe drawers. I thought I might frame that. I could put it in either Clarisse's or the sewing room. Aunt Belle had pleated and embroidered that dress to within an inch of its life. It was all in white. There was a little bundle of felt flowers pinned to it. Such beauty, such love for a baby long ago dead.

I realized I was thinking more and more of living at Aunt Belle's. I was sorting, planning, and placing things in my mind. After all, the place had been my home for a time.

# CHAPTER 17

I had been in all the rooms but Morton's. I didn't really have a reason for not going in there. I just hadn't. I didn't like all the things I had heard about Morton. I never knew him. The stories were just so unhappy.

I had opened the door several days ago to let fresh air in to circulate. The smell had flashed me in the face when I first open the door. It was fetid. I don't know why, but it smelled rank. There were heat and air conditioner vents in the room. I checked and they were open. I knew it got fresh air but ugh. I might have to bleach the whole place before I could stay in there for any length of time.

Morton's door was closed again. I wondered how it had closed. The floors seemed level. I opened it and was stunned with the same stench. It literally took my breath away.

Dust and cobwebs were everywhere. There was the required armoire, bed, and dresser. Morton had a four-stack attorney's bookcase. It was full of books and odd things. I went over to look at it, and my foot bumped something.

There was gopher turtle shell on the floor by the bookcase. The shell looked as if it had been glued together and then shellacked. I had heard Morton liked to hunt and wander the woods. He had probably found that old thing sixty or more years ago. Ramona sniffed at it and made an ick noise. She sat down by the shell while I looked in the shelves.

Randolph leaped in one smooth motion to the top of the bookcase. He was batting something. He knocked it off, and I caught it in mid-air. OH Lord, it was the rattle from a snake. Sixteen rattles. I wonder how things like these and the turtle shell had not turned to dust. They were decades old.

There were a few books on agriculture and business and one book on raising and selling catfish. I wondered if Morton had thought about stocking the old ponds. To my knowledge bream and catfish were about all the fish that lived around here. Most of the books were western stories. I would not mind reading some them myself. I found a couple of Zane Grey westerns.

Maybe Morton had been more interested in the farm and making a life on it more than I thought. Maybe his drunken binges were what had gotten him a reputation of hatefulness. No one would ever know.

Aunt Belle would talk more about Clarisse than Morton. She told me one time she hated to admit it, but Morton was a disappointment to her and Charlie. They had hopes he would grow out of that wild streak and settle down. It was almost a "guilty relief" when he died.

When they brought him home to die, she prayed God would take him soon and put an end to all the misery Morton had caused to himself and others. I didn't know what all misery he had created, but the expression in her face told me it had been a lot.

The chifforobe was empty of clothes. Instead, it held quite an armory. I knew Aunt Belle kept a shot gun propped against the wall at the head of her bed. Uncle Charlie's handgun was in the top drawer of the dresser in that bedroom. Those were all the guns I had seen.

I knew how to shoot, but I didn't know anything about the history or types of guns here. I counted seven side arms. One had a long barrel. I did know it was called a hog leg. It was a big, heavy weapon. The others looked like the guns I saw in the John Wayne westerns. There was a .22 rifle and a sawed off shot gun. The others were different styles of rifles and guns.

I breached the sawed off shot gun and found it was loaded. I was willing to bet all the others would be as well. I didn't know for sure, but I thought old ammunition might be unstable. I had planned to call the sheriff about those shells Tony and I found in the new barn. I would ask the sheriff if he could either advise me on these guns or refer me to someone who could. There was probably a gunsmith nearby.

Morton had been dead fifty something years. I imagine some of those guns were Uncle Charlie's. I would need to research them. Instead of keeping all of them, I would probably sell most of them off. I would keep Uncle Charlie's pistol and Aunt Belle's shot gun certainly. I might have to keep that hog leg.

The old holsters and leather goods needed some tender loving care. Once I got them unloaded, I'd ask Tony if he would help me clean and oil the guns and the leather items. There was an old metal box with gun cleaning supplies on the bottom of the cabinet. The gun oil and all the supplies looked as if they were still useable. I took the stained oil-soaked rag out of the box and threw it away. It helped add to the funky smell in Morton's room. I'd pick up some more oil and some wax for the stocks next time I was in town.

I wondered which gun had killed the other man.

Why did this room stink? It was a little fainter now. Perhaps, I had gotten used to it. It didn't seem as strong. Ramona had jumped on the bed and immediately got back down. I decided I could help with the musty smell if I washed all the bed linens. There was a blue chenille spread and a quilt laying across the foot of the bed.

I took the quilt off Morton's bed and gathered the one from Clarisse's and the other bedroom. I carried them outside and hung them on the line. The sun would help freshen them. I would throw them in the dryer, but I thought the sun and fresh air would be the best first step. I probably needed to run them through the dryer cycles several times to beat the dust out them.

I returned upstairs with a posse of cats. We went back into Morton's room. Nope, it still smelled as bad as before. I thought about opening the window even though the air conditioner was on. I had brought an old candle up with me, and I lit it. I knew candles would pull a smoky smell from a room. I hoped it would help with this odor.

I started taking off the bedspread and lost my breath. The bed was the source of the smell. Good Heavens. What had died in there? Morton, of course. Why did it smell now?

I took the bed spread down and threw it in the washer with a cup of vinegar and a whole cup of Tide. The straight vinegar smelled better.

The cats were standing at the top of the stairs. They would not go into Morton's room now. Randolph had bushed his tail like he did the other night. I wondered if it was the smell or something he heard. He was poised to strike. Ramona had fluffed out as well. She was crouched down near Clarisse's bedroom door. She looked as if she was protecting that room.

I had some big plastic bags in the other room. I had used them to pack up all that cloth    for the church ladies. I grabbed several bags. Holding my hand over my nose, I approached the bed. Both cats remained as they were.

The dingy sheets on it indicated the bed had probably not been remade since Morton's funeral. I lifted the top sheet and saw another. I pulled it back, and in true Alfred Hitchcock manner, I let out a blood curdling scream.

The sheets were stained brown. There were two mice skeletons in the center. Dear God. Morton's dead body had been removed, and the bloody sheets had remained on the bed. His bloody death sheets.

I am going to be sick.

I had to leave the room. I sat down in Ring-a-ding's rocker. The cats followed me. Ramona patted me until I let her get in my lap. Randolph jumped on the bed and starred at me. I think they were as shocked as I was. My heart was pounding, my head throbbing, and I was nauseated. I wasn't sure if it was from the smell or the knowledge of what was there.

Had Aunt Belle known those horrid sheets were still on the bed? Surely not. I couldn't believe she would have allowed those bloody sheets to remain. Belle was pretty fastidious about things being clean. Morton's bed was NOT clean.

The day she told me about Morton having been such a disappointment, she told me Charlie had closed the door after Morton's body was removed.

I wondered if anyone had gone in that room again. I just need to believe she didn't know what had been left. She said Uncle Charlie never entered Morton's room after he died. Maybe Aunt Belle didn't either.

I think that door was closed the day he died and never opened. The smell wasn't in the other parts of the house. It hung in an abysmal miasma in Morton's room. When the undertaker carried Morton's body out, someone threw the sheets over the mattress so the blood would be covered up. No one returned. Old Morton had left a part of himself behind all right, and it was gross.

Girding my loins and trying to hold my breath, I grabbed the plastic bags. No one has ever stripped a bed faster than I did that day. I was going to burn those sheets in the trash barrel right then.

The mattress was stained. That raunchy smell came from it, too. I would need help to get it out of the house. It was going out as soon as I could get Tony to come over. I called him as I watched the sheets catch fire.

"Yes, Ma'am, I can come over in about an hour."

I didn't tell him what was staining the mattress. He looked at it and then at me. "Are those old pee stains? This room stinks."

"I guess. I don't know, but this mattress has got to go. Do you think the two of us can carry it downstairs? I was thinking about burning it because of the smell."

He grabbed one side and I got the other. The old thing just folded up on itself. Tony told me to go get some twine. He thought we could roll it up.

We got it into bedroll shape, and Tony tied it. We each took an end and carried it down the steps. It was not as heavy as I had expected. He put it on the back of the truck.

"Miss Patty, I don't think we'd ever get that thing to burn. I am going to take it to the back of the fields and spread it out. The varmints will tear it apart. They'll use it for nesting and stuff. You don't want the smell of burned feathers up here anyway."

We rode to the very back of the property. I pushed, and Tony pulled until we drug that nasty thing out of the truck bed. He cut the twine and let it flop open. I cringed at the thought of bird making a nest from that stinking, bloody mattress.

# CHAPTER 18

I asked Tony about the guns. I told him I didn't want anyone touching them because I was afraid of the older bullets. Tony said he didn't think I needed to be worried about the ammunition. He would ask his daddy about it though. He said his grandfather, uncle, and daddy messed with old guns. They bought them, repaired them, and sold them. He said his sister handled all the sales. She was a computer geek.

I had to laugh. I had taught his older sister in school. She had her daddy's talents for taking things apart and putting them back together, like Tony did. Her talent was with computers though. She had a pretty good business going out of her house. She designed computer systems for individuals and businesses. She did repairs and taught a senior citizen computer class. She did all the computer work for a couple of businesses, including her husband's. He was an accountant. He took care of Belles' business affairs and taxes, as well as mine.

Tony called his daddy, telling him about the arsenal. His daddy, Darryl, Mr. Melvin, and Tony's Uncle Tim were at the house in no time. We went upstairs. Thankfully, the smell had dissipated some. I had a spray can of air freshener with me just in case though.

"What happened to the mattress?" Mr. Melvin asked. Tony said "We took it to the woods. It was in bad shape."

"It sure smells in here, Patty. Did a mouse die in here?" asked Mr. Melvin.

"I'm not sure, but I think that is what happened. I am going to do a thorough cleaning." I answered.

I grabbed an old sheet from the sewing room. Tim spread it on the under mattress. Darryl took out one gun from the wardrobe at a time. He removed the ammunition. Then he handed the gun to Tim or their daddy to lay on the sheet. Not all the guns were loaded, but several were. Darryl found a couple of boxes of cartridges in one of the drawers.

"I don't think you have to worry about any of this ammo, Patty. It's old, but it has been kept dry. I will put the boxes in the back of our truck and get the cartridges from the barn, too. I'll take it to the firing range where we can get rid of it safely. If you decide to keep any of the guns, I'll get you some new ammunition."

The men continued to talk above my head about the different weapons. They decided they would clean them and assess the value for me. Tim said the three of them tinkered with antique guns and knives. Darryl and Mr. Melvin especially loved working on the older weapons. They had a nice workshop set up in one end of Darryl's electrical shop.

I was so glad they would do an evaluation of the condition and value of each of the weapons. I was totally ignorant of things like that. I asked them to repair anything that needed to be done, also.

I showed them the shotgun and pistol from downstairs. I asked if they wanted to take those two items with them.

"No, Patty, those are in good shape. Belle kept them cleaned and oiled. You don't need to worry about them. Besides you need to keep a gun in the house. You ought to take one of those holsters and wear Charlie's pistol when you go out in the yard."

"Oh great. I am pistol packing mama, now." I laughed. It was true. I needed to carry a pistol outside. I had heard the coyotes and other animals in the woods. With all the farmland being planted in trees, the animals came fairly close to the house. At night, I had to shoo the chickens into their roost to protect them from the foxes and other critters that would kill them. I also knew we had a lot of snakes, many poisonous, in these woods. Snakes were bad to crawl in the hen house for the eggs, too.

I asked about the hog leg. I told them I was kind of fascinated with it. They gave me a history lesson on period guns. The name came from the length of the barrel and the overall size and shape of the gun. Then Mr. Melvin let the shoe drop. The hog leg was probably Morton's gun. He would have liked showing off that big weapon.

I asked if it would have been the one he used to kill the man. "Don't know, child. Possibly. If'n that was his favorite, it mor'n likely was."

EEK. Did I want to keep the murder weapon?

# Chapter 19

Before they left, Darryl and I discussed the condition of the house. "Patty, the place really is in good shape. It is structurally sound. When she had the new roof, heating and air conditioning done, she put in insulation. I rewired the entire house. I'll come back tomorrow, and we'll look over everything. If you want to stay here, I don't think you have anything to worry about."

They carried all the guns off. Tim took all the leather holsters and belts. Tim said he loved working the old leather. "I use my own mixture of oils. It really cleans, preserves and softens the leather. Darryl thinks I ought to patent my special blend." He was rubbing his hand caressingly over the tooled rifle case. Mr. Melvin said years ago there had been a man who made shoes, saddles, and other leather goods in town. He used to do fancy hand tooling on things. He was sure this rifle case was one of his.

Darryl said "Grandma had an old pocketbook the leather goods man made. It was tooled leather. That thing was beautiful. I wonder whatever happened to it."

Tim told him "I have it. I fixed the strap on it. She tore it loose when she fell that last time. Grandma died before I could get it back to her. It is in the cedar chest at home. You want it?"

"No, you keep it. It means more to you because you fixed it. I'd like to see it again though."

They wandered on to the truck. They were still telling stories about the old leather goods man and some of the different pieces he made.

Well, after all that and with the nasty mattress and sheets, I was tired and filthy. The cats I went into the pink bathroom. I turned the water on in the sink so it would get warm. Ramona jumped up and started drinking at the stream. I watched her lapping at the water. I guess I would wait to brush my teeth.

Randolph sat on the toilet seat and washed his face. "Well, Kitties, what do you think? Did we exorcise Morton from the house today? Maybe that stench was his stinky personality. I hope we didn't release him into the house." Ramona looked at me with her big round eyes as if she were saying "Oh, I hope not."

I took a shower and put on my pajamas. The cats I discussed our dinner plans. We decided breakfast was the best answer. I cooked them an egg and one strip of bacon. Refilling their dry food bowl and taking up their wet food dishes from the morning, I thought "Is this home?"

William called. I briefly told him about the nasty mattress. He was curious about the guns. We shared a few more minutes of our day. I told him I was dead-tired, and I planned to go straight to bed. We shared a few more sweet nothings and hung up.

The cats and I went to bed with a deep sigh of relief. I think we were all worn out. I couldn't turn my brain off for sleep though. I was back to thinking if I should sell or stay.

## Chapter 20

During the night Ramona was patting my arm. She probably wanted scratching. I wanted to sleep. I pulled my arm out from the covers and reached for her. She had moved away.

Then she was patting my arm again. I sat up. Ramona was asleep at the foot of the bed. Randolph was curled beside her.

I must have been having a very realistic dream. I finally went back to sleep, but it was restless one.

When I awoke around 3:00 that morning both cats were lying against me. They, too, were awake. I heard a noise from upstairs. Surely, it was the old house making noises, but it scared me and the two not so fearless felines, too.

I probably should have gone upstairs to investigate. Randolph and Ramona seemed as if they really wanted me to stay with them in the bed, so I did the cowardly thing and pulled the covers over my head. Both Ramona and Randolph crawled under with me.

# CHAPTER 21

I slept late the next morning. I didn't hear Guinea Girl's wake up call.

I pulled on my housecoat and started the coffee-my magic elixir. I had gotten the coffee addiction honestly from Ring-a-ding and my daddy. We had to have our caffeine fix first thing every morning. The three of us drank coffee all through the day, too. Ring-a-ding's coffee pot was always ready. When it was emptied, a new pot was perked right away.

The cats and I fixed our breakfast--canned salmon cat food for them and oatmeal with walnuts and cranberries for me with several cups of coffee.

My mind was fuzzy today. I just felt heavy. I really didn't want to do anything but go back to bed. Last night's disturbance was hanging over my head.

I had an appointment with the accountant for this afternoon.

The cats and I did our morning ablutions. I dressed in a lightweight floral sundress with a lavender jacket. I really liked this outfit. Lavender and shades of purples were my favorite colors, just like pink was Ring-a-ding's.

One Easter Sunday we went to church looking like Easter Eggs. She was wearing a bright pink dress with a straw hat. She had hot glued big pink and white flowers on her hat. It was an impressive sight.

I was wearing lavender pants and a matching jacket. The blouse had a yellow and lavender floral pattern. Aunt Belle looked at me and asked where my hat was. I didn't have one. "You need an Easter bonnet."

"I'll just go bareheaded. I don't need a hat." Oops. Wrong thing to say.

"You go upstairs to Charlie's chifforobe. Get that green and white hat box down for me. I'll be right behind you."

There was no sense in arguing. I had no idea what kind of hat she was about to stick on my head, but I would wear it. The church ladies would forgive whatever it was. They would know Belle was behind it.

I put the box on the bed and stepped away. She was rummaging in her humpback truck. In a minute she came out with a yellow silk rose and a lavender scarf.

In that box was Uncle Charlie's white Panama hat. She tied the scarf around the crown allowing it to flow from the back as an extended hat band. Then she put the yellow rose into knot of the scarf. Ring-a-ding slapped the hat on my head. It worked. It was beautiful. Uncle Charlie's hat fit me. "You look killer, Baby."

## CHAPTER 22

Albert, the accountant, was waiting for me. He had pulled out all of Belle's papers he felt I needed to see. "When you leave, you take that accordion folder. I made you copies of all documents and papers I think you should have. About two years ago, Miss Belle started leaving most of the business to me. She'd come to town about once a month. We'd have a nice visit for a few minutes. Then we would get down to it. We'd review everything that had been done or would need to be done about her business. She was sharp as a tack even the last time I saw her. Tony called to tell me she was in the hospital. I grabbed my hat and headed straight there."

"She wanted to talk business. Except for the acre and half that surrounds the house, all the land was now planted in timber. She wanted to be sure I had filed everything for the agricultural tax breaks, and she had paid all the quarterly taxes. I know you were paying everything by then, but I assured her you had done that. Everything was fine."

"This folder has a list of charities she supported. You will need to decide on these. You can continue to give them money or you cancel any or all of them. She did her donations in four installments. The first was in January. The second one was in April. If you want to continue, we can do it the same way. If you do want to support these charities or others, I think the quarterly installments are best. It is whatever you want to do."

"Alfred, I didn't know she did this. I didn't write checks for any of them."

"No, I took care of this. Every year before Christmas, we met so she could decide on what groups needed help. She would figure out how much she would give each one. I sent that amount to them and put it on her donations account. Look over the list, Patty."

All the charities were related to either church, animals, or children. "Aunt Belle's been doing this for years? I guess these places rely on this money. Will I be able to continue this? If I can, we could do the same thing she did at least for this year. This is a lot of money, Alfred." I knew I looked overwhelmed. I was overwhelmed.

"I don't think you truly understand your financial position, Patricia." Alfred told me. "You are now quite wealthy. Unless you do something really stupid, you have more money than you will ever need."

"Oh" I said, numbly. "Oh."

"I'll have a complete accounting for you in a week or so. After you get the death certificate and Letter of Testamentary, we'll meet again, and I'll give you a grand accounting. You won't starve, Patty." Alfred looked at me with such sincerity. "You have plenty."

"Um, keep doing the charities then." I lamely said. "In the same amount as you and Aunt Belle had decided. I guess."

"She gave me several envelopes. One was the property deed to the cemetery. Your family has been buried there ever since Middle Ground Church and the cemetery was built. I had no idea there were deeds to the family plots. That is this envelope." On the front was written in her copperplate script: *Middle Ground Cemetery.*

"The second envelope has a key to the safety deposit box. She has a list of what is in the box there for you. Miss Belle was the most organized person I ever knew. She really didn't need me to do her paperwork. I think she wanted me to double check her. She was always right. I believe she knew the tax codes as well as I did. Maybe better." Alfred said with a laugh.

"This last envelope just has your name on it. I never heard her call you Patricia. It was always Baby, but she wrote Patricia on this. She told me to give you this. It was sealed when she handed it to me. I have no idea what is in it. Do you think Miss Belle had any big dark secrets?'

I thought of Morton's room and shook my head no. "I hope not. If she had any secrets though, they'd be doozies."

He covered all this year's tax matters and gave me copy of everything. "As soon as you get the Death Certificate and Letter of Testamentary, bring them to me. I will make copies. Then I'll help you take care of transferring everything to your name. We'll set a date and go to the courthouse. Do you have any questions?"

I explained about the blue truck and Tony. I told him Tony and I were going to transfer the title into his name this Friday. Alfred reminded me I had to wait until I got the Letter of Testamentary and had probated the will. After that, I would be legally able to change ownership of the truck to Tony.

I asked about Tony's educational fund. Alfred explained Aunt Belle had taken care of Tony by setting up an account through the state's post-secondary educational fund. It was fully funded. Alfred had been instructed to oversee the trust fund for Tony, too. My name would be added when I got all the papers. He said there would be more than enough money for Tony's education. Aunt Belle left him enough to set up his own business or to buy a house if he wanted after he finished school. Alfred had put copies of those instructions in the folder for me, too.

"She loved that boy, and he loved her. He'd bring her in to see me every time. Then he would go out in the lobby to wait for her. He'd sit out reading a paperback book and eating his ice cream."

"They always went to the Dairy Queen before they came here. She had her Peanut Buster Parfait with extra hot fudge. Tony had the biggest chocolate cherry Blizzard they made. She would have Tony bring me a banana split every dang time. Miss Belle was a pistol. God, Patricia, I miss her."

"So do I, Alfred."

# CHAPTER 23

After leaving Alfred I went to the bank. Until I had the necessary papers, my name couldn't be put on all her accounts. I asked about getting into the safe deposit box even though I was sure I couldn't. The teller couldn't help me. My signature wasn't on the card. The bank president who was one of the Deacons of the church, came over. "What do you need, Patricia?"

"It's nothing urgent. Aunt Belle had a safety deposit box, and I just got the key. I was going to look in it, but I don't have the Letter of Testamentary or the death certificate yet."

"Come on over to my desk, Patricia. I know all about this. I need you to sign a new card. When you get the papers, bring them to me. We will reassign the box into your name. Do you need to get into the box today?"

"No, Sir" I answered. "I just got the key. I didn't know she had a safety deposit box. She left me a list of what is in there. I don't think it's anything I need. I have lived without Uncle Charlie's pocket watch and chain all these years. I can live without them a few more days."

# CHAPTER 24

I went by the Funeral Home and paid the bill. I had meant to do that the other day. I hadn't remembered it. I guess I just didn't want her to be gone, so I kept forgetting it. Thank goodness, Mr. Wagner hadn't come after me for non-payment. I would have hated to dig up Ring-a-ding to return the coffin.

I ran by Home Depot. I needed a small vacuum cleaner. Aunt Belle's little handheld one had given up the ghost a year or so ago. I had not been able to find one light enough so she could use it. Most had been a too heavy for her to hold. She had really gotten weak in the last year. I had been doing the cleaning downstairs for her, anyway. "Don't fool with that mess upstairs. Come have a cup of coffee and visit with me."

I found a handheld vacuum cleaner. While I was looking, I saw a canister vacuum with long and short hoses. There was a big heavy Hoover upright at Belle's place. I bought the handheld and the canister. I could leave the Hoover downstairs. The canister vacuum would be good to have upstairs and to use on the steps. There were a lot of cobwebs in the upstairs rooms. The dust was thick, too, especially in Morton's room. I dreaded going back in there.

Next, I stopped by the grocery store and picked up a few things. I needed something that would do heavy cleaning and pick up all that dust. I got a supply of spray bleach and Windex. I had already used up all Aunt Belle had. I found some oil soap for furniture. I hope I would not destroy anything. Maybe this oil soap would cut through the years of dust and dirt.

I was talking to a lady in the aisle about what I was cleaning and the condition it was in. She recommended I get this specific polish for the furniture. She told me to wash the wood with the oil soap. It had to be rinsed thoroughly and then dried with a towel as completely as possible. I was to put a fan in the room to help circulate the air so the wood would dry out more. "Let all that moisture get out of the wood or you'll ruin it." She warned me. I was to wait a day or two before polishing. "Put it on. Let it haze over and buff it until it shines."

I guess I knew what I would be doing for the next several days. I wondered if I could get Randolph and Ramona to brush down cobwebs with their tails.

# CHAPTER 25

That evening I was brushing the cats on the back porch when I remembered the letter in my pocketbook. The three of us retrieved it. I sat down at the kitchen table. I was looking at the oil cloth covering this old farm table. I told Ramona it needed replacing. I asked if she had any favorite colors she would like. She looked at me and purred. I took that to mean anything but pink.

I got a glass of sweet tea and opened the envelope.

*"Dear Baby,*

*Well, I said I wasn't going to go, but I guess the Good Lord and Charlie decided differently. I really don't mind. This has been a hard year for me. I have had Charlie coming more and more often in my dreams. He was ready for me to come home. I was ready to go, too.*

*There wasn't a better man than your Uncle Charlie. I have missed him every day. While I still could, I went up to our room. I would lay down on our bed. I'd just talk to him like we did before we went to sleep every night. I recounted the day's activities to him. I felt like he needed to know what was happening in my life and yours, too. When I couldn't go up the steps anymore, I did the same thing on his bed downstairs. I didn't tell people because I didn't want them to think I was a senile old woman. Besides, it wasn't any of their business.*

*Remember Charlie saying "Ain't nobody's bidness but my own"? He tickled me. He was a good man. MY good man.*

*I want you to know that I have appreciated all you and your parents did for me and Charlie through the years. Your daddy did as much to keep this house up and going as anyone did. His handiwork can be found in every room. Your mama was like my own child. When Louisa and Eli died, she just became mine. I was proud to have her.*

*I felt so bad for you when your mama and daddy were killed in the wreck. You had always been my baby, but I decided then, you and I would be each other's family forever. I guess we already were.*

*I hope you don't mind that I put everything on you. I don't have anyone else. I know you will look after Tony and be sure he is okay. He's the only other person that means anything to me. This last year I couldn't have done without him. You had your job and William. Tony would come after school and help me. He came most Saturday's when he should have been out with his friends.*

*Make sure he gets his education. Alfred has an account set up. You'll need to get your name on it. It will pay for Tony's schooling and help him get started in life. When he turns 25 or so, whatever you think is best, give him the rest of the money. Make sure he gets the blue truck, too. I picked that boy's brain clean to find out everything he would have on a truck. I called the Ford place and asked to speak to Derrick Branch. I told Derrick everything that Tony had said, and I wanted the truck in Tony's favorite color, blue.*

*Derrick called me about a week later and said, "Miss Belle, I got your truck for you. What do you want me to do with it?" I told him to bring it to the house just before school got out. Tony would come here right from school. Tony thought I had company. There was a car to take Derrick back to town and that shiny blue truck in the yard.*

*Tony came in the house, and I asked him "What do you think of that fancy truck, Young'un?"*

*He just smiled and said "That's a beauty. Mr. Derrick, you do have a good-looking truck. Can I look at it?"*

*"Tony," I said. "That is OUR new truck." I wish you could have seen that boy's face. We got in it and went to town. He showed that thing off.*

*I wish he would have taken it then, but he was too proud to accept it. He loved it though. He drove it and kept it pretty.*

*Baby, I just wanted to tell you again that I love you. I want you to have everything that I got. There will be enough money for you to live on for the rest of your life. Don't let any man take any of it though. I watched what Charlie spent and what he spent it on. I handled the money all our lives. You do the same.*

*My dream is for you to teach as long as you want and then retire to follow your dreams. You have always talked about traveling and maybe writing a book. I think you should. You got the money now, and you are young enough to pursue your dreams.*

*Thank you, Baby. I love you.*

*Ring-a-Ding"*

# CHAPTER 26

I cried myself to sleep that night. I think the letter was the icing on the cake. All the emotions and fatigue just collapsed on top of me.

About 3:00 that morning I sat bolt upright in the bed. Again, I thought Ramona was patting my arm. She wasn't. She was standing on the foot of the bed, fluffed out to twice her size, staring right at me. Randolph was crouched down as if he was going to attack something.

There was that sigh again. It felt as if someone had been sitting on the bed and then stood up. I felt the mattress give with the shift of an invisible weight.

No one, except the cats and me, were in that room. I grabbed Aunt Belle's shotgun and got up. Flipping on the lights, I saw the room was truly empty.

Wait, I heard a door close. It was not from outside where maybe the wind might rattle the door on the crib. It was in this house.

Randolph and I ran to the top of the stairs. Clarisse's door was closed. So was Morton's. I had left all the doors open to help circulate the air. The windows were closed. There was not a draft to shut the doors. Had I closed the doors to those rooms earlier and just not remembered it? No, I hadn't. I purposefully left them open.

I opened Clarisse's door and peered in. It looked just as I had left it. I placed a book against the open door so it wouldn't close again.

I went to Morton's room to do the same. When I opened the door, the room looked as if it had a haze in it. Not really fog, just not clear, and the smell was back—with a vengeance. This stench was going to send me back to my house in town.

As I stood there, the room seemed to clear. It was as if the vapor was settling into the center of the bed's under mattress. Maybe it was just my eyes being foggy from my abrupt awakening. I propped the door open with a book. Hopefully, the smell would fade.

I was going to add finding a company to "de-skunk" Morton's room to my to-do list.

Maybe a ghostbuster, too.

# CHAPTER 27

I kept waiting for a pat or a noise for the rest of the night. Nothing else happened. I thought if I didn't get more sleep here, I was going to have to go back to my house every night and then drive back here to work at Ring-a-ding's every morning.

The next morning the cats and I dragged ourselves to the kitchen. I told Randolph I appreciated his efforts to help upstairs, but to where had he disappeared? As soon as I opened Morton's door, Randolph vanished. Some protector. At least he tried to come with me. I guess that was an act of bravery. I wasn't feeling very brave.

I looked at my to-do list and crossed off the few things I had accomplished. I decided I was going to clean Morton's room today. If a good cleaning and washing didn't get rid of that smell, I would have to find a fumigator.

Gathering up all my cleaning things, I traipsed upstairs. The doors were still open. Morton's room looked clear and not hazy. I could feel my heart beating. I realized I was afraid of his room. No one had been in it since he died, but I was frightened. Even the cats didn't want to enter. Taking up their posts on her bed, they ran over to Clarisse's room. The little china headed doll and her Bible were between them.

I pulled the lace curtains down. I put them in the washing machine with a lot of vinegar and Tide. I had not brought the quilts that had been airing upstairs. Instead I had put them through several cycles in the dryer. Then I folded them, placing the stack in the front room. The stale smell had dissipated from the fabrics. I had burned the feather pillows when I did the sheets. Tony was right. You don't want the smell of burned chicken and goose feathers around.

I opened all the drawers and found them mostly empty. There had been a couple of pairs of overalls and some shirts. There were two nightshirts in one of the drawers. I held one up and thought Morton must not have been a tall man. Maybe he was a small man with a Napoleon complex. I threw everything in the burn barrel. There was nothing of fabric left in the room.

I thought I should have burned those curtains. It was a waste of time to wash them. My first instinct had been to save not destroy. If I had been thinking, I would have realized the curtains would probably dissolve in the machine. I would have shreds not curtains.

# CHAPTER 28

Sure enough, when I went back to the washing machine, I had strips of lace. I pulled them out and hung them on the line to dry. I'd throw them in the burn barrel later.

The room still smelled but nothing like before. I decided everything in his room that could hold fragrance was leaving this house.

I placed all the books from Morton's shelves in a cardboard box. I put the gopher turtle shell, a couple of malicious looking knives, and all his trinkets into another box. I moved the cartons out on the back porch. I laid all the books open on the floor. I hated to burn the books, but if they still had a smell, they were going up in flames.

Using the canister vacuum cleaner, I got all the cobwebs down. I brushed the walls and vacuumed the floor and baseboards twice. I had brought my steam cleaner from home. I scoured that floor. I'd repeat it all after I washed the furniture.

Filling a bucket with warm water and Murphey's Oil Soap, I headed upstairs. I brought enough old rags and towels to wash and dry everything. I was determined to cleanse this room of the essence of Morton.

The cats still wouldn't get on the under mattress. I planned to ask Tony to help move this out into the back field as well. I was sure it retained a good bit of the odor. If I kept Morton's bed, I would need a new mattress and box spring set for it. Maybe I would sell it or give it away. I didn't think it was very pretty, and it was associated with Morton. Yep, it was going out of this house.

The furniture in this room was not as pretty as that in the other rooms. Aunt Belle and Uncle Charlie had one of those old-fashioned high headboards. I thought I remembered her telling me it was Eastlake style-dark oak with lots of elevated sections and crowning. It was the size of a double bed.

Morton's bed was iron. The head and foot boards were just a square shaped design. Nothing was very pretty about it. The wardrobe was dark. I believed it was pine. There was a dresser in the room, too. It didn't really match the chifforobe, but it was the same color of wood. There was a mirror attached, but the silvering was splotchy with age. I think the bookcases were mahogany. They were the nicest pieces of furniture in his room. I hoped I could keep them.

I started on the bureau. As I wiped more dust off, I saw deep gouges and cut marks in the surface. Morton must have beat this with a belt buckle or something like that. It was so pitted and bruised. I wasn't sure the finish would ever look decent. Talk about anger issues!

It took me two hours on that one piece. I had to refill my bucket three times with clean water and soap. My arm was killing me, and I probably needed to rinse it again. I had taken the drawers out and set them up on newspaper. I had washed them inside and out. I bet I got enough dead spider bodies to fill a coffee can from the inside of the dresser drawers.

I couldn't get behind any of the furniture to clean. I needed to pull the body of the cabinet out from the wall. I would have to make a trip into town to get those slider things movers used. I couldn't budge it. I also thought I would get more Murphy's oil soap, too. I was going through this stuff. This was a good excuse for going to the Piggly Wiggly. I had a hankering for their chicken salad.

I had taken all the curtains down in the other rooms, upstairs and down. They were all lace. I washed and bleached them. Most of them were still quite beautiful. I had laid a clean sheet on the settee. I folded the curtains. Leaving them on the sheet, I draped another clean sheet over them, the freshly aired quilts, and the bedspreads. I had washed all the linens, too. They were there as well. The room was filling up.

I needed to work faster. I had so much physical stuff that had to be done in the house. Once the death certificate and the Letter of Testamentary arrived I would have several days of business to handle.

I needed help. The windows needed cleaning. All the furniture, especially upstairs, needed washing and waxing. I still hadn't gotten through all the drawers downstairs. I was feeling overwhelmed.

I called Tony and told him about the stinky under mattress and what I had been doing. I asked if he knew of anyone that would like to make some money cleaning the windows and all the windowsills. All the baseboards needed cleaning, and the walls needed to be wiped as well. I wanted to steam clean all the floors, too.

Tony said he'd call his best friend Hal. Hal had already offered to come help. Hal's sister Trina would probably come, too. He would come in the morning. He and Hal would get the under mattress out. Tony said he would help me move all the furniture away from the walls. His daddy had some of those furniture mover slides. He'd bring them and a set of hand trucks of his daddy's. "Hal and me can move anything. Miss Patricia, I can wash windows, too. Whatever you need, I will help you do. You know that."

# CHAPTER 29

I ran to the grocery store and got the chicken salad, a set of furniture movers, and enough food to feed Pharaoh's Army. I knew if Tony and Hal were coming, they'd eat as much, if not more, than Pharaoh's Army.

I picked out pieces of chicken for the kitties while I ate my dinner. With full bellies, the cats tended to their washing up. We crawled into Ring-a-ding's bed. The night after the boogie man slammed the doors upstairs, I moved to her bed from Uncle Charlie's. I could have just as easily moved the shotgun, but I didn't. Maybe the hoo-doody wouldn't find me in the different bed.

I think the kitties were happier in her bed, too. We had gotten used to sleeping together by now. Randolph had a habit of laying his head on the other pillow and then stretching his body out the length of the bed. He looked just like a human in that bed. He even put one arm out over the sheet. I took a couple of pictures of him with my phone. No one would believe this cat.

Ramona balled herself up and got beside me. It didn't matter where she lay, she just had to be touching me. That was comforting. She was warm, too. It was nice she had made me a warm spot when I crawled into the bed.

3:00 am. Damn.

Either I had a spook upstairs, or I needed to WD-40 this whole house. Squeaks, footsteps, sighs. I kept dreaming someone was softly whispering to me.

Well, the shotgun and I headed up the steps. The cats followed but remained a safe distance behind me. When I got to the top of the steps, I peered around the door at Morton's room. There was the mist again and the smell. It was faint but growing stronger. Suddenly, the book I had used to prop open the door was kicked into the hall. Morton's door slammed closed.

I don't know who hit the ground floor first--me or the cats. I can promise you one thing. All three of us were shaking. I had two giant puff balls looking at me. Bright yellow eyes were wide. My hair was standing on end, and my blue eyes were just as wide as theirs.

I didn't even change my clothes. I grabbed those two felines, and we went to my house in town for the rest of the night. I may have set a world speed record getting home.

# CHAPTER 30

Reluctantly, the cats and I went back to Ring-a-ding's the next morning. When I tell you we moved cautiously into the house, I mean we were slower than any turtle. Both cats stayed behind me. Where were those fearless felines you hear about?

I fed the cats and made coffee. I was nervous and discombobulated. I was not going upstairs alone.

Tony, Hal, and Hal's sister, Trina, came in. They sat down for a cup of coffee and some toast and fig preserves. I felt better having them in the house.

We mapped out our day's strategies for the house. We had the sliders. Trina had brought a box of latex gloves. I should have used gloves yesterday. The first order of business was to get that old under mattress out of the house. The boys took off to do that. They said they would wash the windows. They would let Trina and me do the furniture. That way if the furniture got ruined, it wouldn't be their fault. They were laughing as they went upstairs.

I slowly followed them. The cats decided they wanted to go outside for the day.

The door was closed. The book was still lying in the hallway. "Miss Patty, did you mean to leave this book here?" asked Hal.

I sucked in a deep breath and lied. I really didn't want the kids to think I was a fruit-loop. I just told them I must have dropped the book. "Why'd you close the door? This room needs all the fresh air it can get." Tony asked.

I agreed with him. Again lying, I told them I must have closed it out of habit. Hal opened the door and walked in. I was holding my breath.

"It doesn't smell so bad." Hal told Tony. "You said it smelled like someone had died in here."

Thank goodness. Maybe things were improving, except for that temper tantrum last night. That wasn't an improvement. That scared the pee-turkey out of me and the cats.

I was beginning to believe Morton was mad because I had invaded his room. He was really going to be ticked off when I got rid of everything of his in that room. I had decided on the way over this morning all the furniture and anything I could find in that room would be out of this house.

Before the boys took the mattress, they pulled all the furniture in Morton's room away from the walls. They carried the under mattress out to the back field. Tony reported the other mattress had already been gutted. Most of the feathers and stuffing had been carried off. I felt sorry for any offspring lying in that disgusting mess.

I started back on the bureau, and Trina began cleaning the drawer surfaces on the chifforobe. The drawers weren't bad. I guess being upright they didn't get as much crud collected on them. She rinsed them and dried them really well. Then she put the drawers in the hallway and placed a small oscillating fan nearby to gently circulate the air around them.

# CHAPTER 31

Both Hal and Trina had been my students. She and I chatted about school and the different events. Hal played football and basketball. Trina had fallen and injured her left knee at Christmas. She hoped she'd be able to play softball and basketball next year.

It was quite an enjoyable day. I had forgotten about the fears from the night before. The cats had come in with Tony and Hal. They were supervising the window washing in the two upstairs front rooms. I could hear the boys laughing and talking. I was so glad they were here.

I asked Trina if she and Hal could come back the next couple of days. She said she'd ask her folks, but she thought they could. Hal would start football practice in another month. That was all they had pending.

With the help of these three young people, I felt like we were making some progress. Trina had washed down the iron bed. It now looked white instead of yellowish-ick.

"I love this old bed. I am saving up money to buy one. My bed doesn't have a headboard."

The light bulb flashed. "Do you like the style of this bed, Trina? It isn't very fancy."

"Yes'm. I do. I don't like all the curly-ques. I like straight lines. I think they look clean and uncluttered."

"Oh, I have to agree about the uncluttered look. I love all the curlicues though. Trina, I am not going to be able to keep the furniture in this room. Would you like the bed? I would like for someone who loves it to have it."

"Miss Patty, I don't think I have enough money yet to buy it."

"Oh no, Honey, you don't understand. It is yours to take. You ask your mama and daddy if you can have it. If they say yes, the boys can take it to your house and set it up. "

She beamed. I beamed. I may have just gotten rid of Morton's bed. I hope Morton didn't go home with Trina though.

She said she'd ask her parents about the bed. She thought it would be okay with them. She was redecorating her bedroom this summer. I told her there was no rush. If they wanted to see the bed first, that was fine with me. "Oh please, let her have it." I thought.

The boys finished the windows in the sewing room. We stopped for lunch. When everyone was "full as a tick" as Uncle Charlie would say, it looked like a bunch of buzzards had cleared the table.

While we ate, we talked about any number of things. The boys were teasing each other and slipping pieces of ham to Randolph. Ramona was taken with Trina. I pretended not to see Ramona lying in Trina's lap at the table. Trina was feeding little pieces of ham to her.

We returned upstairs, kitties in tow. Tony and Hal wiped down the walls and washed the baseboards in the sewing room. It looked so light and smelled so fresh. I had thought I would need to repaint these rooms but perhaps not. The wide baseboards were bright white. I could not get over how great they looked.

Before Trina and I started on the body of Morton's chifforobe, I asked the boys to pull the dresser, bed, and the chifforobe further into the room. I wanted to get behind them to clean the walls, baseboards, and the back of the furniture better than I had.

Nasty was not the word for it. Trina wrote her name in the dust on the wall behind the wardrobe. "Miss Patty, has this room ever been cleaned?"

"Not in a long time." I laughed. If she only knew. There was stuff besides goosal-feathers and dust bunnies stuck to these walls and furniture.

I walked behind the dresser with my dust cloth and was wiping it down.

There was something under the dresser. The edge of something was just sticking out enough to catch my rag.

We tipped it over on its back and found enough spider webs to weave a rope from here to Augusta. There was also a thin piece of board nailed to the frame. Hal ran down to the kitchen and grabbed a hammer and screwdriver. He popped the wooden cover off to reveal a little pocket between the two strips of support wood.

A wine-colored leather book fell out. It looked as if it had just been placed there the day before. Tony picked it all up and handed it to me.

We all went into the Clarisse's room where there was better light. The pages had names and numbers written on them. It was a ledger of Morton's moonshine deliveries and the money he had collected. Apparently, the illegal whisky business was lucrative. A few of the family names I recognized. These people had probably been dead nearly as long as Morton. The 'shine probably killed them.

William loved history and mystery. I would show this to him when I saw him Sunday. I would add it to the stack of things going to the historical society.

The book was a little more fragile than I had first thought. The handwriting looked like that of an educated person. The front cover had Morton's name in beautiful script. There was a note "Purvis owes me 10 gal."

Maybe Purvis, the moonshiner, owed Morton ten gallons of whisky. The boys started telling white lightening stories they had heard. Hal said he thought the Purvis farm still made 'shine. He said his daddy told him never to go to the Purvis's place for any reason.

"Mine, too. He said if I had a flat tire in front of their house to just keep on driving and not stop at the Purvis' for help." Tony explained. "Daddy said old man Purvis was a mean son of a b…. He was really mean." I smiled to myself over Tony's courtly behavior.

Not to be outdone, Trina jumped in "You know Trudy Purvis, Miss Patricia?" I nodded yes. "I heard that she sleeps around. The reason she didn't come back to school this year was that she got pregnant." Unfortunately, I had heard the same story.

I told them to go on home for the rest of the day. All three of them had put in a full day of work. I was tired, too. We'd get started again in the morning.

I called William that night earlier than our usual time. I told him about last night and the book incident. He had to work the late shift at the drug store. William asked if he could come out and spend the night. I was sorely tempted, but I was a school teacher. I didn't need any scandal attached to my name. Thank you very much.

He wanted me to come back to my place for the night if he couldn't stay with me at Aunt Belle's. William got off at 4:30 the next day. He would come on out to Belle's place as soon as he could get away from work.

I appreciated his concern. I was staying the night, and that was it. I promised to call him if I had goblins visiting during night.

# CHAPTER 32

Safely tucked in bed, the cats and I fell asleep in our now accustomed places. If they were as tired as I was, the haints could dance on the bed and we'd not know it.

"Sigh."

What?

"Sigh."

Crap!

I felt a soft touch to my cheek. "Mama?"

I think I wet my pants.

"Mama? Mama? Wake up, Mama."

"What is it, child?" Did I say that?

"It's Morton, Mama. He's come in my room and he's been touching me again. Make him stop, Mama."

If I were sleeping, this was the most vivid dream I had ever had. Randolph was asleep beside me. Ramona was against my leg. She hadn't moved. I could feel a soft, sweet breath on my face.

"Clarisse? Is that you?" I asked in a whisper.

"Mama. Wake up. Make him stop."

I tried to reach for her, but I didn't feel anyone or anything. "Clarisse, get in the bed with me." I felt the bed sag as if she had climbed in.

I wasn't scared. I felt an overwhelming sense of protectiveness. I guess we were really and truly haunted. I wondered when Ring-a-ding would show up.

I slept soundly the rest of the night. If Clarisse were there, she was no threat.

I made the bed the next morning thinking "Did I dream that?" I touched the side of my face. I knew it had been real. That young girl had thought I was her mother. She had come to me for help. Did I do what Aunt Belle would have done? Tucking the child into bed with her and Uncle Charlie? It seemed to be the right thing at the time.

## CHAPTER 33

I had a call notifying me the death certificate and Letter of Testamentary had arrived at the funeral home. I promised Mr. Wagner I would come by that afternoon for them.

The kids showed up about 9:30. Tony and I had a ritual. Having breakfast or coffee and toast with jelly or preserves while we planned our day. Hal and Trina just fell into step with us.

"Can we look at the book while we eat?" Tony asked. I told him I had left it upstairs where we were. He said he'd run up and get it.

"Miss Patty. Where did you leave the book?" he called from upstairs.

I told him I had left it on the dresser in Clarisse's room. "No, Ma'am, it isn't there."

We joined Tony in Clarisse's room. True enough it wasn't there. I didn't remember doing anything with it. I had not gone back upstairs after they left.

We searched every room upstairs. That book was not there. The boys even tipped the dresser over again and checked the hidey-hole. Nothing.

All I could do was tell them it would show up. I must have done something with it and not remembered. I thought to myself, if Clarisse can come to me in the night, Morton could dang well hide a book.

# CHAPTER 34

I told Trina to help the boys downstairs. They could do the windows and baseboards there. I didn't want them upstairs alone. I didn't want to be upstairs.

Moving back to town was looking a lot better this morning.

I picked up the documents I needed. I took copies to the bank where everything was completed so I could take over Belle's accounts. One of the cashiers printed copies of all her savings and checking accounts. There were two savings accounts. She had several CD's and Money Market accounts I had not known about. No wonder the old girl never worried about money.

I was taken into the safety deposit room. The cashier and I opened Belle's vault. She removed it and led me into a small private area where I could go through it. I didn't want to leave the kids at the house too long.

I scooped everything into a Piggly Wiggly bag. Then I stuffed it all in my peacock printed tote bag to take home. It looked mostly like land deeds and some contracts on the cattle and swine they used to raise and sell. I had her list. I didn't really need to go through it all at the moment. I could take my time at home.

Sure enough, there was Uncle Charlie's watch and chain. I think they called that style pocket watch a turnip because it was so big and heavy. There was a $20 gold piece hanging off the chain as a fob. He wore it in the top pocket of his bib overalls. I remember seeing that chain and the gold piece glisten in the sun. The watch was in one pocket, and there was a clip he attached to the opposite strap of his overalls.

I stopped at Colonel Chicken and bought dinner for us. Those young'uns were eating me out of house and home. It was cheap pay. They would not take any money from me. They told me wait and pay either at the end of the week or when all the jobs were finished. Feeding them was the least I could do every day.

Those three had done an amazing job on the front room. All the furniture was pulled away from the walls. The backs of all the pieces had been wiped clean of dust. The windows sparkled. Tony had washed the outside while Trina did the inside. Hal had vacuumed the walls and floors. He had started washing the window frames and baseboards. They had almost completed the entire room. "Miss Patty, we brushed the walls down first. Then we vacuumed the floor before we got started on anything else. Isn't that what you told Tony and Hall to do upstairs?" asked Trina. Obviously, Trina was the one in charge of the work crew today.

Trina didn't know it yet, but she was running for Student Council in the fall. I needed her leadership in the group I sponsored. I knew she was good student. She was well-liked, an athlete, and a leader. Yep, she was running. I'd start planting that seed today.

"Alright, you buzzards. Dinner is served." After eating, it did look like a horde of vultures had cleaned the table. Randolph and Ramona had eaten so much chicken their bellies protruded. They had gone to bed. I didn't expect to see them anymore that day.

The kids returned to the front room as I straighten up the kitchen. I filled Ring-a-ding's water pitcher and began tending to her extensive flower collection. I looked forward to getting the windows in the kitchen cleaned. The shelves were glass. I remember when Daddy did those for her. She had talked about wanting some shelves to hold her African Violets. He fixed her up. He installed three glass shelves across the kitchen windows. Each one spanned the eight-foot width of the windows.

Ring-a-ding could root anything. In the old warmer oven of the wood cook stove was her indoor plant supplies. She had a fertilizer spray for the orchids, blue granulated fertilizer for the violets, and a jar of rooting hormone.

Philodendron trailed along the top shelves. She had rooted more in old water pitchers placed on top of the old stove. I bet one or two of the vines were at least six feet long. Several times a year she'd cut the vines back to about two feet foot in length. The cuttings would be trimmed to two feet and then put in water to root. Everyone who came to the house was offered philodendron that she had rooted.

I counted sixteen African Violets. There were five orchids. One of the white ones had blossoms. Placed in several little Philadelphia Cream Cheese glasses were violet leaves. Across the top of the small glass, she put tin foil, poked a hole in the foil, and popped in a violet leaf. Voila, two weeks later—roots appeared.

Over the years I had quite a collection of her philodendron and violets. I loved the orchids, too. I would buy them for her when I saw a particularly lovely one. She had stair step shelves on the front porch and an identical set on the back porch. From spring until just before frost, her indoor plants lived on the porches. Almost every room in the house had a peace lily. She swore the lilies cleaned the air. I'd put one in Morton's room soon. Maybe I'd put two.

Each June after school got out, I would spend a couple of days with her and her "indoor garden." We divided and replanted everything that needed it. There were several begonias that were a fiery orange. She said the original plant was her mother's. I had one. Several of her friends had them now.

We had the old Gum Swamp Orchid, which was really a Walking Orchid. Ring-a-ding's mother had dug it up in Gum Swamp and brought it home. I had two that were huge at my house. She had two more. There were a couple of buds on her plants. They would have blooms in a few days. The blooms made a root ball like a spider plant. There were now a number of those in town, too. She was generous with her plants.

While the kids laughed and worked in the front room, I moved all her indoor plants to the two porches. I watered everything and picked the dead leaves off them. They all looked really healthy. I was glad. If I had neglected her flowers, Morton, the poltergeist, would be the least of my worries. Ring-a-ding would come back and get me.

# CHAPTER 35

William came about 5:30. We decided to go into town to a family style buffet restaurant. I didn't have much in the house to fix after the kids went through like a cyclone. He did not particularly want picked clean chicken bones or a peanut butter and jelly sandwich.

He had run home from work to shower. He had changed into an aqua blue golf shirt. It was beautiful color on him. His black hair gleamed in the light, and the blue showed off his olive skin.

I had slipped on white pants and a floral top that had an aqua and white pattern. We pointed at each other. "Great minds think alike." We said in unison.

Being a weeknight, the restaurant wasn't as full as the weekend. A number of people came by and spoke to one or both of us. Because of our work and of course, I had grown up here and taught here; we knew most everyone in town. This was a blessing and a curse. Mostly our food got cold while we chatted with people.

After the kind souls had faded away from the table, I told William about the house. "William, there are some strange goings-on. I know Clarisse is there. I think the smell and the noise is Morton. I believe Morton is a hateful, vengeful soul. I don't believe in ghosties and ghoulies and things that go bump in the night. At least, I didn't. I surely do now."

"Move back home, Honey. I worry about you in that old house. Everyone knows you are there by yourself. After all this hoo-doody stuff you've told me, I don't like you being there at all." William had taken my hand and shook his head.

"William, I have not really been scared, except that night Morton had the temper tantrum and threw the book. I was scared then, and so were Ramona and Randolph. You should have seen us leaving that house. I had a cat under each arm, and I was in my nightgown. We looked like a streak of lightening coming out that front door." I giggled.

William came back to the house with me. We explored both floors. The odor in Morton's room was very faint. "I think this is a good sign. The smell is fading. Maybe Morton is going away." I said wishfully.

"Maybe Morton is just saving up for the next big fight!" William opened his eyes, so they were big and round. "oooo—WEEE—oooooh," he sang while wiggling his fingers ghoulishly at me.

"Stop that. Don't do things like that and then leave me here alone!" I laughingly punched his arm.

"You don't have to be alone. I can park the car behind the new barn." he said wiggling his eyebrows Groucho style.

A few more sweet nothings and a couple of kisses were exchanged. The car wasn't visible from behind the new barn.

# CHAPTER 36

"What in hell is that?" William sat up in the bed, scattering cats across the room.

Sigh. It was 3:00. "Morton is ticked off again, or maybe it's Ring-a-ding. She'd be mad that you are here and in her bed. "

William pulled on his pants and grabbed Belle's shot gun. He was headed up the steps before my feet hit the floor.

"William, there won't be anybody there." I yelled up the steps.

"Oh-my-God." I heard William retch. "Is this the smell you were talking about?"

"Yeah. It is really awful. See, you gave him the idea today to save it all up and blow it at us tonight. I think this must be the smell of brimstone. What do you .....? Look! Look! See the haze. It is settling at the center of the bed."

The fog began to intensify over the bed center. Then it dissipated completely. I didn't know about giving this bed to Trina. Maybe we should take the frame out in the woods and leave it with the mattresses.

"Do you know old lady Gemma Larkin?" I think you need to call her. Let her try to run Morton off. She's the closest thing to a witch we have in town."

"Miss Gemma isn't a witch. She uses herbs and stuff. She's just a little bit looney-toons. She gets confused and talks to her dead relatives. She's been that way all my life." I told him.

We all crawled back in bed. Sleep didn't come easily, but the night passed pleasantly.

When I woke that morning, I smelled coffee. The cats were gone. There were noises upstairs.

William was dismantling Morton's bed frame. "If he is connected to this bed that he died in, I can take care of that. It is going out to the crib. He can haunt that old barn and leave you alone."

I laughed. You had best get going. The kids will be here in about thirty minutes, and you have to go to work."

"No, I am off today. Harry needed me to cover for him, so he is taking today for me. I brought all my work clothes from the car when I moved it around to the front yard. I am legitimately here to help my girlfriend with her spooktacular house."

I had to say I was grateful.

Breakfast was ready when the kids came in. "Mama sent you this. She said she knew we were eating you out of house and home. The least she could do was refill your jelly and preserves." Said Tony.

Trina sat a wicker basket on the kitchen table. "Mama made brownies for her Bible Study group. While she was at it, she made these apple and cinnamon muffins. Daddy has been asking for them. She made extra and told me to bring them to you. I think Mama is glad for us to be over here and not at home."

Hal immediately took one of the muffins and spread butter on it. "MMMMM, still warm. Nobody cooks better than our mama."

"Don't' you ever say that in front of my mama. The only person she thinks cooks better than she does is Grandma." Tony warned his friends.

# CHAPTER 37

William and the boys carried the old bed frame out to the crib. I told Trina I wasn't sure she needed that old bed. We'd have to see. You could tell she was disappointed, but I didn't want to tell her a ghost might go home with her.

The kids continued their work in the front rooms. William and I went upstairs. I showed him everything. We looked in Belle's scarf trunk. I had glanced in there but hadn't taken anything out. I saw a tissue paper bundle and lifted it out.

The handkerchief baby quilt had 36 lovely floral handkerchiefs. A few of them had initials embroidered. I recognized Ring-a-ding's, Louise's and their mother's initials. The backing was embroidered table runners. The runners had floral designs. Ring-a-ding had taken lavender, purple, and white variegated crochet thread to create a lacey edging connecting the handkerchiefs. She had trimmed the border with a fancy pattern. It was museum worthy!

I was showing it to William. He picked up a white envelope that had fallen from the folds.

*"Dear Baby,*

*I think this little lap piece turned out well. I used all of Mama's hand-kerchiefs I could find and then I filled in with those Louisa and I had done. I wish I could have tatted the edges, but my eyes just wouldn't let me do that kind of small work anymore. I can crochet with my eyes closed, but I can't tat anymore.*

*The back is two of Mama's table runners that she had made for her dresser so many years ago. After she died, I took them. I laid them out in the yard with a little lemon and vinegar water on the dark spots after I washed them. The sun lightened the stains right up. Those old runners have her favorite flowers on them-daffodils and iris. Purple and yellow were Mama's favorite colors, just like they are yours…*

*You remind me of Mama in so many ways. You talk with your hands just like she did. You have her blue eyes, too. I wish you had gotten to know my mama and daddy. You would have loved them.*

*I want you to put this little pretty up. I made it for that great-great-grand-something or other you will have one day. I wish you'd gotten on the stick and found you a man, so I'd have that great-great to hold. But you didn't. Don't wait a lot longer, Child.*

*I love you, Baby,*

*Ring-a-ding"*

I started laughing and handed William the letter. He read it and looked at me. "Have you ever thought about getting married, Patty?"

"No, not really. I don't think my biological clock has had its alarm turned on. Have you ever thought about it?"

'Yeah. I have." Said William as he walked out of the room.

That was it. All that was said. Huh?

# CHAPTER 38

"Miss Patricia! Would you come down here?" yelled one of the boys.

William was standing in the left front room with the boys. They had steamed the floors and were trying to put the furniture back in place.

The old organ weighed a ton. I didn't know it was actually two pieces screwed together. Hal had a screwdriver. He wanted to take the top off so it would be lighter and easier to move. Trina was arguing against it. "You might not be able to get it to fit together again. Then what will you do?"

"Do we need to separate it? I was going to take the back off. The old bellows don't work anymore. I thought I would look at them. They are made of either leather or canvas. I don't know if they can be fixed, but maybe someone can." I explained.

William took the screwdriver and removed the back panel. Dear Lord. Here was another spider home-cobwebs and bodies. One living spider tried to escape. Trina screamed and Tony stomped on it. "My hero" She swooned before breaking into giggles.

I was thinking there might be a little romance brewing between Tony and Trina.

Hal and I cleaned out the back of the organ. The bellows were shot. Mice and age had taken care of them years ago. There were three or four pages of sheet music trapped inside and one forlorn dead mouse. I guess Randolph and Ramona had been doing their jobs. I hadn't seen any live mice.

William and Tony emptied out the compartment behind the music stand. Trina carried the sheet music and a couple of books over to Uncle Charlies' desk.

MARLENE RATLEDGE BUCHANAN

The old top didn't want to come off the base. The years of varnish, dust, and dirt had glued the two pieces together. William and Tony worked silently at the welds.

"Honey, this is beautiful wood. Why don't we refinish it? If we can get the billows fixed, you could play it. Couldn't you?"

I noticed the three kids perking up at the "honey" and the "we". I knew William and I would be the talk of the town by nightfall.

"I haven't played the organ in years. The organ and the upright piano are what Aunt Belle taught me on. I am pretty sure it would come back to me. She gave me the old upright piano when I moved into my own place. I have it at home, but I rarely play anymore. It used to sit on that far wall in this room. This organ was her wedding gift from her grandparents. I would love to restore it. There is so much more that needs to be done first that I can't think about restoring the organ right now."

"I bet Mr. Casper would be interested. Truth be known, Mr. Casper would love to work on this. He still does some small projects for people. He hasn't had anything like this to do since I moved in. Miss Rachel would probably give me six months free rent if I could get him involved in something that took him out from under her feet." William laughed.

William called Mr. Casper about the organ. About thirty minutes later he and Miss Rachel drove up to the house.

"Let me see that old pump organ. I remember it. Umm-hmm. Belle used to make that thing sing. Umm-hmm. Yeah, umm-hmm. Yeah."

William and Mr. Casper stayed in the front room "um-humming" over the organ. Miss Rachel, the kids, the cats, and I went to the kitchen for coffee and muffins.

"If you can get that ol' fool occupied, I'll do anything in the world you ask. That man is driving me crazy. Ever since he retired, he hasn't had enough to do. He stays right where I am. I've been cooking sixty years for him, and he ain't never complained. Now he wants to help. Help, hell. He causes the biggest messes you ever did see. Then I have to clean it all up."

106

We were all sitting at the table eating and laughing when the men came in. "Let me get you a cup of coffee and some of these brownies, Mr. Casper."

"Did you cook these here brownies? I remember when you was a little girl, and you cooked the most God-awful cookies. Your daddy, Charlie and me ate them as long as you stood there. Lord have mercy, it was hard getting them cookies to go down. After we bragged on you and you left, your daddy took them cookies and threw 'em in the hog pen. Them hogs wouldn't eat them cookies either. They finally just got stomped in the slop. You'd used salt instead of sugar. Your daddy just laughed and was proud of you for trying. He looked at me, and he thanked me. 'Casper, I appreciate you going along with that. My baby meant well, but that sure was a terrible cookie.' Charlie was spittin' and laughin' so hard he couldn't get a breath."

I had never known that. Every so often Daddy would tell me how well he remembered my first attempt at baking. I thought it was because it was so good. Daddy was a prize-my prize.

Mr. Casper went into great detail about what needed to be done to restore the organ. He gave us a twenty-minute lecture on what the old finish was and then twenty more minutes on how to remove it. I learned more about cleaning wood than I ever wanted to know.

I gave Miss Rachel some philodendron cuttings. She led Mr. Casper out to their truck. He was still talking about the organ. She mouthed "Thank you. Bless you" over her shoulder.

William and the boys loaded the organ on the blue truck. The three of them took it to Mr. Casper's workshop.

# CHAPTER 39

"Miss Patricia, can I ask you something?" Trina and I had moved to the back porch for some restorative rocking. Ramona was lying like a little baby in her arms. You could hear her purrs across the porch. Randolph had jumped into my lap where I began combing him. His "good vibrations" were strong.

"Of course, you can. What's on your mind, Honey?"

"Why don't you want me to have that bed?" I was expecting questions about William and me.

"Trina, I don't want to scare you. You remember that awful smell in Morton's room?" She nodded her head. "I think Morton is still here. I am scared his ghostly self is attached to that bed. If I give it to you, I am afraid I will be giving you Morton, too."

I had to give her credit. She didn't look at me as if I had lost my mind.

"Why do you think he's still here? Have you seen him?"

I explained about the reoccurring smell, the kicked book, and slamming door. "At night, Trina, when I have heard those noises and I go upstairs, the stench is awful. There is a haze in his room that centers over the top of that bed. It did it last night. Tony and Hal had taken the under mattress to the woods. It was just the empty bed frame."

Trina said "You know my grandma still lives with us. She's been dead something like three years, but she still lives with us. Daddy, Hal, and I have seen her several times. She stands in her bedroom and looks out the window a lot."

"Mama swears Grandma keeps hiding things from her. It took Mama three days to find her wedding ring. Mama always puts it in a little saucer on her dresser. It was gone. Then one day her ring was back where she always kept it. Daddy said Grandma didn't want him to marry my mama. He says sometimes at night he can feel her twist his ear, just like she did when he was a little boy and did something wrong."

"I guess if you took the bed home, your grandma might be able to whip Morton and run him off."

"Maybe. Grandma talked about Morton. She said he was just meanness personified. She went to school with him. She said she thought Morton was murdered in his bed. The doctor said he probably wouldn't ever be right again. Grandma said he 'weren't right to start with'". Trina laughed making quotation marks with her fingers.

"Grandma said her older brother and Morton were good friends. Uncle Johnny had come to see Morton after he was hurt. Mr. Charlie took him upstairs. He said Morton opened his eyes and lifted his hand. He thought Morton was going to live and be alright. The next thing anyone knew, Morton was dead. Grandma said he was murdered."

I didn't know any of this. Aunt Belle and Uncle Charlie spoke so infrequently of Morton. I knew very little about him. I found this all fascinating. "Trina, do you think your daddy would tell me more about Morton and the old days?"

"Well, it was really my grandma and my great uncle who knew him. I'll ask Daddy though. Daddy loves to talk about old times, and I'm sure he has some stories he could share."

# CHAPTER 40

William and the boys came in with hamburgers and French fries. I brought Cokes from the refrigerator for our late lunch. William was laughing at Miss Rachel. He said when he left, she ran out to him and hugged him. She kept thanking him. Casper was in the workshop and happy as he could be. "I promised him I would help him when I could."

"Sure, Son. You can help me. Bring me triple naught grade steel wool. I want you to go to the hardware store and get all these things I got 'chere' on this list."

"You made a very happy couple today, William. I bet you never lay a hand on the refinishing of the organ."

"No, but Miss Rachel asked me what I wanted for dinner tomorrow night. She said she would fix me something special. I think I am going to come out really well on this deal." He was laughing as he went back to the front room.

Trina and I had decided our next task would be to get all the furniture in the two front rooms cleaned and polished. We'd leave the upstairs for the time being.

I would focus my energies on the things stored in the drawers. I had quickly gone through Uncle Charlie's desk, but I needed to do a more thorough search of what was there. The first time I went through I found account ledgers from the 1940's and 50's.

Grabbing a trash can, I sat down at Uncle Charlie's desk. Trina and the boys were polishing the furniture with paste wax and buffing it off. That old wood was gleaming with new life. If I stayed here, I would make this the living room. The old upholstery was pretty faded, but Belle had kept sheets over it. I had beat the sofa and chairs within an inch of life to get a lot of dust out.

Uncle Charlie's desk chair had a piece of fabric on the back. Belle had split a pillowcase and covered it. She used safety pins, now rusted, to pin the edges of the pillowcase together. I pulled it off and saw a navy needle pointed background with blue, pink, and white flowers-so delicate and lovely.

I had looked in the center drawer earlier, but I pulled it open again. There were a few coins and at least fifty pens. Most of them had dried up decades ago. I did find Uncle Charlie's fountain pen. It had a gold nib. The case looked as if it had been made of silver. It was black as soot now. I imagined the bladder was hard as a rock, but I would try to clean the pen. Maybe I could get a new bladder. I'd love to use his pen.

He had little Blue Horse spiral topped notepads. These were filled with notes to himself. "Hog wire, U-bolts, potato slips, Dan's shoes".

Dan was the huge work horse. His stall was in the new barn. He had deluxe accommodations. That room was kept spic and span. All his harnesses and bits were hung on the wall. Every item was cleaned after it was used. Dan was brushed down. I remember him standing next to the well. Somebody was lathering him up with soap. Dan hung his head down really low, so his head and ears got a good washing. That horse had such personality.

My fondest memory of Dan was being on his back. Daddy was holding my left leg, and Uncle Charlie had my right. Dan was a big horse, but he was as gentle as anything could be. Daddy was leading Dan around in a circle. Uncle Charlie was telling me to hold on to his mane. I was probably three or four. I still have a little "broom" that Uncle Charlie made for my dollhouse. He had tied some string around some of Dan's mane and given it to me. It looked like the old straw brooms they had used to sweep the yard.

Being in the house was bringing up so many memories.

# Chapter 41

After everyone had gone home, I bathed. Ramona got her fill lapping at the bathroom sink. Randolph attacked the belt from my house coat. I ate my staple peanut butter-blackberry jelly sandwich with the morning left over coffee. I opened some cat food that smelled awful and thrilled the cats.

We crawled into bed. I was laughing to myself about Mr. Casper and how happy he was. Miss Rachel would spoil William for finding Casper something to do.

Randolph had his head on his pillow, his arm out of the bed covers. Ramona was tucked in nice and tight. We drifted off in a peaceful sleep.

I don't know if I automatically awoke because it was 3:00 or something had awakened me. But it was 3:00 and I was awake. The house was silent. I wondered if Morton had followed the bed to the barn. I slipped on my shoes. As quietly as I could, I went upstairs.

The smell was there again. When I got to the top step, I could see the haze. It wasn't like before. It was in the hallway and gliding itself into Clarisse's room. The smell followed the haze. I stood there. The fog moved out of Clarisse's room into the sewing room. It briefly swirled in that room and then glided into the other bedroom. When it went into Uncle Charlie's and Aunt Belle's room, the mist thickened. It was as if it was condensing into a vertical column, not a fog that was parallel to the floor.

Suddenly an arm like shape jutted out of the column. It slammed into the top of the bed. It hit with such a force I could see the bedcovers move. The arm kept pounding the bed and slamming into the mattress. The smell. Suddenly the smell intensified.

I gagged. I couldn't help it. I was about to vomit. The column of smoke pulled in the arm and dashed toward me. I was surrounded by the cloud of decay. It seemed to pull all the heat from my body and all my strength. I was retching but couldn't lift my hand to my mouth. My knees began to tremble. I was losing my balance. I was afraid.

The noise that filled my ears almost deafened me. It was not a roar. It made me think of someone taking a hard, deep gasp that lasted forever. It was as if it was suctioning all sound, all air, all heat, and all energy from around me.

I realized I was on the floor. I had just dropped there as the powerful column of foul air left me. I saw it fade into Morton's room. The door slammed.

After a few minutes I crawled to the stair rail. I managed to pull myself up. The old rail was loose. I pulled it away from the wall, almost falling again. I stood with my forehead against the wall, trying to breathe. It was painful to take in air. When I finally got downstairs, I saw only four minutes had passed. Four of the most horrifying minutes of my life.

I thought about leaving the house, but I was too weak. I lay on the bed. The cats came over to me. They got as close as they could. It was as if they knew I was freezing. Suddenly I realized I was crying—trembling and crying.

Enough. William was right. I needed to go back to town. Let Morton have this place.

# Chapter 42

The next morning, I washed the sheets and remade the bed. I had vomited on my clothes. I never realized I had actually been sick at my stomach. I cleaned the landing upstairs where I had thrown up.

I opened the door to Morton's room. "Do you want me to leave this house, Morton? I am going to. I don't have to stay here with you and Clarisse. The cats and I will go back to town. You need to know that if you won't let me stay here, I will sell this house. Your story-your time here- will belong to someone else. They won't be as tolerant of you as Aunt Belle or me."

I knew it was a bluff. Morton had ownership here now that Belle was gone. He was going to run me and everyone else off. I put a few things in my car and got some cat food. Tonight, I would sleep in my bed, and the haints could have this place.

William called. He was getting off early. I told him I was moving back to town that night. I wasn't even sure I was going to finish cleaning the house. I told him what had happened. "Oh, William, maybe I will just put the house on the market as it stands."

"Honey, now you know what Morton is capable of. I think you do need to stop sleeping at Belle's place. I think he is mad that you have opened his room and you've removed the bed. That bed is where he died and where his essence was left. I think that was where he felt safe. The room is his sanctuary. I don't know. He is angry and maybe feeling lost without the bed as his anchor. You saw last night that he can be physical, too."

"Finish all the paperwork. Let the kids keep cleaning. That stuff must be done whether you sell it or not. Miss Belle had some beautiful things.

I know you want to have some of them. Your place is not going to hold everything. You will either have to put it in storage, or leave it in the house. Leave it where it is for now. You are upset, and you are angry at Morton. Go home, and I will meet you there about 5:00. I'll bring supper. We'll talk tonight. I love you."

William was right. He was the calmness in my world. I needed to… what did he say? He just told me that he loved me. That was the first time he had said it. Wow. He loves me. I felt so happy. I loved him, too. Yes, I did love him. I would tell him tonight. I had been dragging all morning and now I was full of energy and the day was glorious.

# CHAPTER 43

As the kids worked downstairs in the front rooms, I completed clearing Uncle Charlie's desk. I didn't find much of interest. It held mostly old receipts for livestock bought and sold. There was a thin phone book from twenty years ago. I looked up my parents' name and address. Uncle Charlie had the minutes from every town council meeting he had ever attended. I thought I would ask the historical society if they wanted those papers and the ledgers I had found yesterday.

I put those things I would offer to the historical society in a box. I moved then to the items that had been in the organ. Most of it was sheet music and practice books. I found my Thompson practice book complete with my youthful rounded signature. There was small box of pictures. It was fascinating to see the various ages of the photographs.

There were two I thought were daguerreotype. They were printed on metal, not paper. The somber faces of the men and women looked as if they had heard the worst news of their lives. One man reminded me of Uncle Charlie. He was a small man with a lean, lanky frame. This man had a beard, but you could tell he was slender. The woman in the chair had her hair parted in the middle and pulled back into a tight bun. She was wearing a black dress with mutton sleeves. I didn't know for sure, but I thought this must be Uncle Charlie's grandparents. The outfits and the style of picture made me think of something from the 1860's or 70's.

The second picture gave me no clue. I could tell both the man and woman had light eyes. She was holding a small child, maybe a year old. The child was in a long dress. It could have been a boy or girl. Boys wore dresses until they were several years old. Even the child had an austere expression on its face. The man had heavy mutton chops. I think he was little on the pudgy side. The woman looked as if she had escaped from a concentration camp.

Several more formally poised pictures were in the box. There was one of Belle, Charlie, Clarisse, and Morton. Clarisse looked like a five or six-year old. She was wearing a little dress with flowers embroidered on it. She was standing next to Aunt Belle. Her hand was on Belle's, which was resting on the arm of the chair.

Charlie and Morton stood behind them. Morton was a much bigger man than I realized. He was not any taller than Uncle Charlie but very wide. He was more muscular. I thought about those wrestlers on television. He was built like them. You could see the strength and power in his body as well as the distain in his face.

In the picture, no one was smiling, but Morton had a hateful set to his mouth. Looking at him made me think of last night. All I could do was shiver. Morton had light eyes. Well, they all did, but his were colorless in the picture. His must have been ice blue.

I found a few buttons and a pencil in the box with some notes and other pictures. On the back of some the pictures were names. Nothing had a date though. I set the box aside. When I had more time, I would research some of this. I had the old photograph album Mama had put together. I thought I might have Aunt Belle's, too.

I realized I had not found the family Bible. It was a big book with a black leather cover. It had to be in the house somewhere.

# CHAPTER 44

I went through all the drawers in that room. I found scraps of papers and some books. One was *The Black Arrow* by Robert Louis Stevenson. I had a vague memory of reading that. There were a lot of books in this house. I know Aunt Belle and Uncle Charlie had both loved to read.

The kids had been cleaning in the right front room. When I walked in there, I was stunned. It didn't even look like the same place. Trina told me she had washed all the sheets covering the furniture. Hal and Tony had double teamed the windows again. The stain glass in the door was so bright. I hadn't realized how dull the colors had gotten. Once again, they had moved the furniture away from the walls and dusted and vacuumed.

I fixed tomato soup and cheese sandwiches for everyone. I had made sweet tea. To me, sweet tea would quench any thirst. It was welcome this day.

We all got in there and tackled the remaining cleaning. The plans were to wax the furniture tomorrow. Aunt Belle used this room for her television. She loved "her stories." *General Hospital* was one of her favorites. She never missed an episode. There was a character on the show many years ago named Althea. She had several cats named Althea through the years.

After Mama and Daddy died, I lived with Aunt Belle and Uncle Charlie. In the afternoons when I got home from school, she would have something ready for me to eat. It might be a fried egg sandwich or cookies. We would take our afternoon "coffee break" to watch cartoons.

In no time at all we finished up. The kids went home. I took a shower and put on clean clothes. I stuffed all my dirty clothes in plastic bag. I would do laundry at my house tonight. I made sure all the doors and

MARLENE RATLEDGE BUCHANAN

windows were securely latched. I left a light on upstairs and one in the kitchen. If Morton wanted to stomp around and show out tonight, he'd do it without me as an audience. The cats and I went to my car.

# CHAPTER 45

William brought Chinese food. I had set the table. We ate almost as soon as he got there. I told him in more detail about last night. He again told me he thought I was right to come back home.

We moved to the den with coffee and some chocolate pudding I had made while I was waiting for him. The cats were washing up after they had talked William out of almost all his shrimp. I was seeing the cats for the manipulative little angels they were.

I turned on some music. We sat holding hands. "You said you loved me today."

"I know. I do. I have loved you from the first time I saw you. I didn't say anything because I felt like you didn't want a boyfriend. A commitment." William was playing with my fingers.

"I love you, too. I didn't really know it until today. You said it, and suddenly it was like everything fell into place. I love you, William."

"Did you know that Miss Belle called me out to the house to ask what my intentions were?"

"What? No. Did she really?" I smiled.

"She did. I told her then I loved you, but I didn't think you knew you loved me yet. I told her I wanted to make a life with you when you were ready."

"Miss Belle gave me her blessing. She also told me not to wait too long. You might wander away from me if I didn't tie you down."

"Oh, William, I can hear her now." I laughed.

Then he dropped to one knee. "I do want to spend my life with you. I want us to make a life together. Please, marry me?"

I was speechless. I looked at him. We had only declared our love for each other that day. I felt as if someone had shoved me. I fell forward into his arms. I kissed him and murmured "Yes, William, let's start a life together."

After some cuddling, he reached into his pocket. He pulled out a little velvet bag. "I have been carrying this for months. You don't have to accept it. You can pick out whatever ring you want, but Miss Belle gave this to me when I told her I wanted to marry you. It was one of her rings. She said to offer it to you but to tell you that you didn't have to take it. You can reset the stones or keep it in its current setting. If you don't want it as an engagement ring, then you can do what you want with it."

Of course, I wanted Ring-a-ding's ring. It seemed right I should wear it. I loved all her old Victorian and Art Deco style jewelry. This was white gold with a lot of filigree. There was an old fashioned mine cut diamond in the middle. It was a huge stone. There were smaller diamonds set around the base of the elevated center stone. I could vaguely remember her wearing that ring. She had not worn it in years. I think it had gotten too small for her. She wore three rings on her left hand and two on her right-- Charlie's wedding band, her wedding band, a cameo carved with a woman standing, a pink tourmaline, and a little silver bee on her index finger. I had created that bee in a jewelry making class when I was in college.

When Uncle Charlie died, she put his wedding ring on her left thumb. When the funeral director took her jewelry off, he handed everything to me. I slipped Uncle Charlie's wedding ring on my left thumb, where I wore my daddy's wedding band. I placed Ring-a-ding's little band on my right pinkie finger, where I wore Mama's wedding set. I had kept the other pieces in the little bag I was handed. There were locked in a box in my closet.

## CHAPTER 46

Ring-a-ding had been a small woman with tiny hands. I hoped the ring could be resized. It was too small for me. With all the filigree and details, I was afraid it would not lend itself to being enlarged.

William and I agreed I would take it to the jeweler in town the next morning. We also decided to keep the engagement secret for a few days. Just our luscious little secret.

I was surprised at the number of people in the jewelry store. I waited a few minutes while the others completed their business. I looked at all the rings in the cases. There was not one ring that was more beautiful than Ring-a-ding's.

"Hey Patricia, how are you doing? I hear you're working on fixing up Belle's place. Is there much to do? Are you going to move in or sell it?" Mrs. Taylor laughed. Mrs. Taylor was always laughing.

"Hey, Mrs. Taylor. I don't know what I am going to do yet. The house is in really good condition. I am just cleaning and thinking about adding a bathroom. I have been so busy since Aunt Belle died. I didn't realize how much there was to do following a death. There is a lot of things to take care of. Some days I think I will move into Belle's place, and other days I think I need to stay where I am and sell the farm. I wonder if Mr. Taylor would look at this ring. Do you think he can resize it enough to fit me?"

"Why, that's Belle's diamond ring. I wondered about it. It wasn't on her hand at the funeral. Bill, come here."

Mr. Taylor came out from the back of the shop. "Patricia, what brings you in today?"

I showed him the ring. I asked if he thought it could be resized.

Turning it over in his hands, he said "How much bigger do you need it?"

Mrs. Taylor held out the circle of ring sizers and reached for my right hand. I pulled my right hand back and put forth my left.

"What? Are you engaged to William? Oh, lands' sake, that is the best news, and you are going to wear Belle's ring." Mrs. Taylor was all over me, hugging, laughing, and telling me all about the stuff I would need to do for the wedding.

Mr. Taylor took over and measured my ring finger. Then he measured Belle's ring. He examined the ring with his loop. He held the ring at arms' length and looked at it. Then he started scrutinizing it again with the loop. "Yep, Patricia, I surely can make it fit you. I am going to cut it here and splice in a band of gold. I can keep all the detail work like it is. I'll clean it and tighten up all the prongs. You want me to do an appraisal on it for insurance? You need to be sure all her jewelry is insured. This is 18 Karat gold, and it is really old. It is older than Belle. I bet you this was her mother's ring."

I knew it was pointless, but I asked if they could keep the ring and the engagement a secret until I had the ring to wear. Mrs. Taylor used an imaginary key to lock her lips and then tossed the key over her shoulder. Mr. Taylor pulled an imaginary zipper across his mouth. I figured I had fifteen minutes before it was all over town.

## CHAPTER 47

Alfred and I walked up to the courthouse to probate the will. He had the paperwork drawn up to complete the transference of all properties to me. He had told me he would help with everything. I would not have to have the lawyer involved. I was glad.

That afternoon, Tony and I went to the tag office. I changed ownership of the blue truck over to him. I don't believe I had ever seen a boy prouder of anything.

I asked him if he would call Trina for me. He did.

"Trina, have you talked to your mama and daddy about that bed?"

"Yes'm. They said I could have it. Morton isn't attached to it then? I am supposed to pay you for it. How much do you want?"

"No, I don't think it was the bed that held Morton. I think it is just the room. If he does show up at your house, we'll take the bed to the back field, and let it rust away."

"If you can't accept it outright, then consider it partial payment for all the work you have done. Do you and Hal want to meet Tony and me at Belle's place this afternoon? The boys can take the bed to your place and set it up for you."

About an hour later, she and Hal drove up the house. As the boys put the bed frame into Hal's truck, she told me she had set up sawhorses outside. "I am going to paint it. It will be light blue. My curtains and bedspread have blues, purples and pinks in them."

I told her I thought that would be beautiful. I hoped she would enjoy her new bed. "Be sure to invite your grandmama in to see it—just in case Morton is with it. She'll put the fear of God in him."

# CHAPTER 48

I went on in the house after they left. It was nice to have the house quiet. I did miss the cats. I let the chickens out and fed them. Guinea Girl was happy to see me.

I unloaded all the sheets from the dryer and folded them up. The two front rooms were almost finished.

The plastic bin that Ring-a-ding had used to hold all those Humpback trunk papers was upstairs. I got a trashcan and went up. Morton's door was closed.

"Hey Morton, I'm here. Take your stink and leave."

The tub held nothing of importance, really. I set aside some things I thought the historical society might be interested in. I would take them downstairs and put them in the box I had designated for that.

There were a few letters. I read them. I didn't know these people, but a couple of envelopes contained notes of condolence on Clarisse's death. Belle had tied them with a pink ribbon. There were no notes about Morton's passing.

I found a heart shaped candy box with a red satin rose on it. "I love you more today than the day we wed. Charlie." In it were a few things of his, some notes to each other about their love, a little crocheted cross intended as a book marker, and a few pictures. One was of Charlie's prize bull, Bully-Boy. He had won every prize at the fair. Bully-Boy's blue ribbon was in the box.

In the bureau in Clarisse's room, I found the family Bible. I realized I had not turned out the drawers in her room. I had put the kids to working downstairs because of Morton's bad behavior. We still needed to finish upstairs.

I sat down in the rocking chair and opened the Bible. It was the King James' version. The color plates were still vibrant. I flipped though looking at them. I found a little dried rose between two pieces of paper in the center. There was a slip of paper stuck between the pages. "Clarisse's rose."

I wondered if this was one of the funeral flowers or if it was just a rose bud Clarisse had picked. Whatever meaning the rose had was now gone forever. It obviously had been important to Ring-a-ding. I replaced the delicate flower between the pages.

There was a family records page. It listed the wedding date of Charlie and Belle. Ring-a-ding had penciled in Uncle Charlie's date of death. Morton's birthday was recorded as was his death date. No other information on him was included. Clarisse's information had been put in as well. Hers had an annotation she died from scarlet fever and pneumonia. The penmanship I thought was Uncle Charlie's copper plate script, but it might have been Belle's. People were taught to write so beautifully back then. I had tried to copy their style but was no match for that gracefulness. I added Belle's death date.

I fell asleep rocking. I felt the pressure of Ramona crawling in my lap. I kept dozing off and on. Ramona was so light.

I woke up and looked at Ramona in my lap. It wasn't Ramona. It was Clarisse's little china and satin doll.

# CHAPTER 49

It had been Clarisse in my lap. I felt calm and at peace. I hoped she did, too.

I rounded up the chickens. I shooed Guinea girl into the hen house with the chickens. I grabbed some cat food and headed home.

The cats kept sniffing at me. I finally sat down on the couch. Ramona and Randolph crawled into my lap. I told the kitties what had happened that day. Ramona curled into a tight ball and lay her head on my arm. Randolph lay beside me and purred loudly. I just sat there with them thinking about what a pleasant experience I had felt in Clarisse's room. The three of us stayed that way until William called.

We caught up on the day's events. I told him how good I had felt when I woke up with Clarisse's doll in my lap. "William, I think Clarisse believes I am Aunt Belle."

"I do think she believes you are Belle. I think Clarisse sees you as the person to take care of her. Bringing you her doll and curling up in your lap says she trusts you. Don't you agree?"

"I think you are right. I don't know how to reassure her that I will do all I can. Maybe she already realizes I am standing up to Morton. She probably needs me in Belle's place." I answered.

I asked if he had heard anything about our engagement. He had not. Mr. and Mrs. Taylor had indeed zipped and locked their lips.

William would pick up the ring when it is ready. He said he wants us to parade all over town showing off. Laughing, I agreed that was just what we would do.

The ring would be ready on Saturday. I asked if he wanted to wait to Sunday to show it off. "Yeah. Let's do that. You get dressed up, and we'll go to church. I bet it won't be two minutes before your ring is spotted. We are telling the world on Sunday." We both just laughed with pure joy.

I couldn't wait until we could make the announcement.

"When do you want to get married?" he asked.

"I-I don't know. I hadn't thought that far ahead. When do you want to?"

"Let's talk about it tomorrow. I will be at Belle's place about 5:00. Okay? I'll bring dinner. What are you going to work on?"

I explained the kids and I needed to finish the upstairs. After that, I really wanted to start on the kitchen. I had talked to Darryl earlier that day. He declared the house in great shape after he had gone over it with a fine tooth comb the day before.

I wanted William to help me make plans about the kitchen. The appliances were replaced in the remodel eight years ago. They were white, but the walls were pink--Pepto-Bismol pink. Linoleum had been put on the heart pine floors originally. When Belle had redone the house, she had left the linoleum alone. It was dark brick like pattern. I wanted the original floors if they could be restored. If not, I would find a light color to replace the linoleum. I added a note to ask Mr. Horace about the kitchen floor.

"I'll be there tomorrow, and we'll talk. I can take a day off next week if you want to go look at paint, cabinets, and flooring. Are you moving into Belle's place? You know it does have a past."

# CHAPTER 50

We ate dinner and laughed at how happy Miss Rachel and Mr. Casper were. William had bought all the things on the list. He had helped Mr. Casper lay the top of the organ on a pair of sawhorses. "You won't recognize Mr. Casper. He is spending his days in his workshop. You can hear him whistling. I have never seen the two of them happier. He was in the workshop. Miss Rachel was humming in the kitchen."

William took measurements of the kitchen. Whether I stayed or not, I needed to replace those dark brown cabinets. I would go with white. The resale value will be better with white. It would certainly make the room look larger and brighter. I didn't understand why she used that dark brown on the cabinets and baseboards.

A second-floor bathroom would have to be added. I would prefer to put in closets, but I guess the house had armoires in every room for its lifetime. It could continue with them. I didn't really know how one could add closets in this house. I had been playing with the idea of turning Morton's room into a full bath and closets. I didn't know how I felt about getting naked in a bathroom that might still contain Morton.

We walked upstairs to mildly foul-smelling air. We looked at Morton and Clarisse's rooms. William was drawing on a note pad. "I think you could take this part of Morton's room for a bathroom. This would be over the kitchen. Water and drains could be added here. If you use Clarisse's room, you'll have to add a lot more plumbing. You might have to add another septic tank." William walked, measured, and drew plans on his pad.

"Do any of these fireplaces work?" he asked.

I explained when Belle put in the air conditioning and heating systems, she had the fireplaces closed off. I wasn't sure, but I thought everything was sealed so a fire couldn't be burned in any of them ever again. They were just for looks.

"What if you took the fireplaces up here out? You could take the ones on the first floor out, too, if you want. You could make corner closets in each room. The space would be triangular, but that could be fixed with the carpentry. A good carpenter might be able to do more with the space than I can see right now. He could square up the corner. The floors would have to be put in where chimney is. If that part of the floor is in a closet it wouldn't show so matching the wood wouldn't be a big problem." William continued to measure and mutter.

This was a possibility. I had not thought about demolishing the fireplaces. I could leave the fireplace in the front room. That was the only mantel that was sort of pretty. It had been painted brown for some reason. The rest of the mantels were just utilitarian, a shelving board with a little cornice to hold them in place. We went back downstairs discussing the possibilities.

"Honey, let's talk dates." He took the calendar off the refrigerator. We sat at the kitchen table with our glasses of tea. William and I began talking about all the things we needed to do. I started making a list of possible dates for when we could get married. He wanted to marry as soon as possible. I felt as if I needed a little more time. I had so much to do with Belle's place. I hadn't even been engaged 24 hours.

I thought I had taken care of most of Ring-a-ding's business. I knew other things would come up, but I felt confident the most critical issues were handled. I did need to decide what to do about the house. I was again thinking of staying here. I just didn't know if I could live with Morton. Clarisse wasn't a problem, but Morton surely was.

The sensible thing for us to do would be to move into Belle's place when we married. It had eight rooms. My little house was truly small. We certainly could live there. It would be close to our work, but it would be tight.

"William, would you want to live at Belle's place? What about Morton? I think he is here to stay. He hates me, and I don't think he is real fond of you either."

"Maybe we can get a Catholic priest to do an exorcism. Now, don't laugh, Patty. I'm serious. I never dreamed I would be sharing space with a ghost. You see these priests on TV doing exorcisms and the demons leave. It might be worth looking into."

I stopped laughing and looked at him. "You know, maybe we really should call in a professional, like a priest. It would be worth a try. If all else fails, we can board up Morton's room again. We would just pretend that space doesn't exist. That's what Aunt Belle and Uncle Charlie did for over a half century."

We kissed good night...several times. Then we left for our respective homes.

Randolph met me at the door. Ramona was on sitting on the fireplace mantel. I heard the "Well, it is about time" in their voices.

After they ate, they joined me in the den, and we watched a little TV. I told them we had to make some big decisions soon. They were getting a daddy, and I was getting a husband. They weren't very interested.

# CHAPTER 51

I had hired a man to bush hog everything that wasn't planted in pines. That was mostly the little field behind the new barn and along the drive and roadway. He was hard at work when I got to Ring-a-ding's. Normally, I only have to open the car door, and Randolph would step out, look around, and go to the front door. Ramona hesitates and then follows him. The noise of the tractor and the bush hog must have been frightening to them. They refused to leave the car. I picked them up in my arms and carried them into the house. Even inside, they hesitated to leave me. I didn't realize the noise would be so disturbing to them. If I had, I would have let them stay at my house in town.

Everything downstairs looked fine. I did dread going up to Morton's ghoul center. The cats led the way. They would take a few steps, look back to see if I were following, and then go up a few more steps. We finally reached the landing house. Yep. Stinky. Morton's room looked the same. The smell was in all the upstairs rooms, not just in his. I had to wonder if Morton and a skunk were related. How did one person, uh ghost, produce so much vile aroma? My eyes were tearing as I entered the poltergeist's room.

I put my hands on my hips in the Wonder Woman position and said loudly "Oh, Morton, grow up and go away." Then the cats and I stomped downstairs.

I was so frustrated with the smell and Morton that I wished I could have picked him up bodily and thrown him out the door. Mr. Herman had given me the names of people who could advise me on an upstairs bathroom and closets. I just didn't know if I could let anyone work up there with Morton. I was afraid he would run them off.

I stomped back up the steps. "Morton, you and Clarisse can stay, but you have to cut this crap out. I know you can control this smell and your behavior. I saw you having a temper tantrum in Belle's room. You are acting like a two-year-old."

The smell worsened. I went back downstairs. My temper tantrum didn't do any good, but I felt better anyway.

# CHAPTER 52

"Patricia, it's Alfred. Would you do me a favor?"

"Of course, what do you need?" I asked.

"I am merging your files and Miss Belle's. Quarterly taxes will be due in a couple of months. I can't find the paperwork on the trees last planted. Also, there should be a lease agreement for last year. She let Bob Porter put his goats on the back field. I need that for the agriculture tax filling. Do you have it? I was certain I put one copy in your folder, and I had kept a copy. We file this every year. It isn't critical that I have it now. I just need to have copies when we do your taxes. I just want to get everything pulled together now while I have the time. Once tax season is here, I am swamped."

I hadn't seen anything like that. I told him I would look in the folder he gave me. I may have gotten it by mistake. I promised to call him back in a few minutes.

I had to think. In all the turmoil I couldn't remember where I had left the folder Alfred had given me. Ah yes, it was on the floor in the hanging side of Belle's wardrobe. When I pulled it out, I saw my peacock patterned tote bag. I hadn't gone through the safe deposit stuff either. I was falling further and further behind on my schedule. I need to evaluate what I needed to do, what I wanted to do, and what I could put off for several days or weeks--maybe months.

The cats and I carried everything to the kitchen table. I took everything out of the folder and looked at the pages. There both documents were. Alfred had clipped them together. They had accidentally got attached to my copies.

I called Alfred. I would bring the papers to him that afternoon. I know when you are working on something and can't find that one thing you need, it will drive you crazy. Actually, I think I was standing in my own crazy right now.

Simultaneously, there was a knock at the front door and at the kitchen door. I opened the kitchen door to the bush hog guy. Tony, Trina, and Hal came traipsing into the kitchen from the front of the house.

Tony grabbed the coffee pot, Hal grabbed the cups, and Trina opened a grocery sack of her mama's muffins.

I invited Mr. Otis in. Tony sat a cup of coffee down in front of him. Hal put the carton of milk on the table. Trina put a muffin on a plate and handed it to him.

"You shore got good help, Patty. I ain't never had no better service than this." Mr. Otis was laughing, showing his toothless grin.

"I think the kids are ready to move in and move me out. They have been helping with all the sorting and cleaning. I couldn't have done anything without them." I was bragging on them right and left, and it was true. I would still be rummaging through drawers without them.

Mr. Otis went through the entire southern ritual of "How you doing? How're your folks doing? Did you hear about so-and-so?" Then everyone asked him about his family and his business. It is just southern something we do. It takes a while to say hello and a while to say goodbye. We just accept it and think nothing of it. When all that was completed, I made an agreement with Mr. Otis he would bush hog that back field and the shoulders of the road twice a month during the summer.

"Patty, did you know there is an old shed in the very back of the new barn lot? You know where them pine trees start and the lot ends? It's real growed up back there."

"No sir, I don't remember one. I haven't been back there in a long time. That field was kept clean for the cows. Aunt Belle hasn't had cattle back there in years."

"No, Child, you're thinking about the part of the back lot where the creek and watering hole is. You walk back up to the left to where them old pens were. That part ain't in pines. It was just growed up with trash trees, black berry vines, and stuff. I had my old bush hog on the tractor. I couldn't get all the way up to it, but I cut up as far as I could. I'd forgotten that old shed was there until I hit one of them fallen down fence posts. It could be cleared up, but unless you really need it, I'd leave that mess alone. There's no telling what lives in that there tangle of briars."

I had no idea there was a shelter or pens there. "We can leave it all in scrub. It isn't any use to me. Mr. Otis, what do you think that place was used for? I had no idea it was there."

He started laughing. "'Riginally, they pulled cows out to the pens to check them over. I imagine that's where Morton hid his car. He hauled 'shine. My paw said Morton and Jonah Purvis hauled 'shine for Jonah's paw. I heared some more stories 'bout Morton and Jonah from my paw. Them's two were rounders, fer sure."

Well, maybe if I could get some moonshine up to Morton, he'd be nicer to me.

# CHAPTER 53

I hated to leave Uncle Charlie's watch in the vault forever. I could remember sitting on his lap and listening to it. He would make it chime for me sometimes. I wonder if I could get a glass box of some sort to display it. I wound it a little, and it began ticking. It was big old thing, but maybe William would like to wear it. He always wore a white lab coat at work, but he sometimes wore three-piece suits. He could wear it for dress up. I thought about getting him a pair of Uncle Charlie's bib overalls. I knew he would never wear them, but he'd be cute if he would.

Dana called. She had my teddy bear of Belle's and Charlie's clothes ready. I told her I would pick it up when I came to town that afternoon. She sent me a picture on the phone. It was adorable. She had made the head and upper body out of Belle's violet patterned dress. The lower part and the legs were Uncle Charlie's overalls. She had even added a bib to the pants.

Trina came in. I showed her the picture of the bear. "I love it. I wonder what we have of my grandma's that we could use to make us one. Maybe if Mama had one made out of Grandma's dress, she would leave her alone. Would you send me that picture please?"

"I heard you talking about putting in a bathroom. I thought we probably should have waited until that was done before we did all this cleaning. It will be a royal mess when you start that." Trina was sending the teddy bear picture on to someone.

"I know, but Trina, it had to be done. I'll cover everything with sheets. Maybe the cleanup won't be too bad." I told her what William and I had discussed about an upstairs bath and closets.

"Do you know Christine Young? She moved into the old Dillion house. You need to go see it. She did something like that. Do you know where she lives on Pike Street? I think she put a pantry in the kitchen where the fireplace was. Her house is only one story though. She took all the old bricks and made walkways in her flower beds. The house is really cute."

# Chapter 54

Sliding the contents of the safety deposit box back into my tote, I replaced it in Belle's chifforobe. I told the kids I had to run to town for an hour or so. My janitorial crew was hard at work.

Dana's house was lavender with cream shutters. In the front was a cream picket fence with a sign on it. The Crafting Ladies with an email address and phone number on it. Someone had painted a little bear and a rabbit in purple and pink calico on one side. The other side had a matching elephant. The yard was tidy and had azaleas in front of the house. In the window boxes, Dana had put pink and white begonias.

Dana opened the door before I could even knock. "Come in. I hope you will love her as much as I do." She pulled the bear from where it had sat on the couch. Adorable was just not descriptive enough. Dana had an extra piece of tatting from the dress. She had tied it around the bear's head. Stuck in the bow knot was a small spray of violets.

"Miss Patricia, would you let us use pictures of your teddy bear on our website. It has all the right colors, and she has so much personality. This was the first time I had made one using two different fabrics. I think it works so well."

I told her she could use it for anything she wanted. I was tickled to death with it. She showed me through her house. One room was used for cutting and storing fabrics. The second was for assembly of the creations. She had huge rolls of batting material. Her bedroom would become the assembly room. She would make a show room in the former assembly room. While she was looking for some old pieces of furniture to use for display, I asked her to stop by and look at the furniture in Morton's room. She could have the chifforobe and the dresser if she liked.

She told me about her forthcoming wedding. Her plans were to turn this house into her business and retail shop. She and her new husband would be moving into one of the new houses being built just outside of town.

My next stop was to drop off the papers to Alfred. We chatted for a few minutes. Then I ran to the bank to cash a check to pay the kids. At the grocery store I loaded up on monkey food for the kids. I believe all three of them had a hollow leg. I had never seen so much food disappear so fast.

I drove by Christine's house. She was home and working outside in the flower beds. I pulled into her driveway.

"Hey, Christine, how are you doing? I see you have the house finished."

"Well, hey yourself. How've you been doing? I heard you were moving into Miss Belle's place. Are you doing a lot of renovations? Get out and come inside."

I explained the kids had told me about her remodel. I wondered if I could see it.

"Of course, I am tickled to death to show it off. I am still trying to do a little bit in the garden using the old fireplace bricks. That is what I am doing today. It is really too hot to be laying bricks. I am glad you stopped by. I needed a good excuse to stop." She said with a huge smile and giving me a hug.

We walked through the house as she explained some of the work that had to be done to make the house safe. "We didn't know there was so much damage as there was to the underpinning and supports. The whole back porch looked safe, but it wasn't. Horace and his crew pulled that whole porch off, which was hardly attached at the base. We had a huge bonfire. It was a little termite bar-b-que. Horace called the fire department. They used it as a practice drill. I think most of the town came to see the blaze."

"Christine, I think I want to make the back porch of Belle's place into a sunroom like you did. Do you have separate heat and air conditioning units for it? I want something like this, but I am afraid it will be too hot."

"My sunroom stays fairly shady during the hottest part of the day. I think it will get a lot more sunlight in the fall and winter. You'll have to talk to someone who knows about yours, but I only have the one set of heat and A/C units."

I told her that I was thinking of using Mr. Horace to do all the work on the house. She explained he and his crew did an excellent job. "When they finished every night, they left it pretty picked up and clean. I was really pleased. I wasn't living here while they were doing all the renovations. Each time I stopped by everyone was diligently doing his job. You can trust Horace to do things well and treat you right."

We continued to talk about friends and her house. It was a neat layout of five rooms, and the sunroom was perfect.

"Patricia, would you do me a favor?"

"You know I will. What can I do for you?"

"Do you still have some of your Aunt Belle's philodendron?"

I had to laugh. "Yes, I do. Do you want variegated, solid color, small leaf, or large leaf? She has it all. It needs thinning out. How much do you want? Anytime you are out that way, just stop and I will load you up with a mess of it. If you want, I can drop you off a bunch at your house in a couple of days."

We agreed she would get some pretty vases or interesting containers together. She'd call me when she was ready. ow much do yoyou want?

After a quick stop at Colonel Chicken, I headed for home. I had enough chicken and side dishes for 14 people—or Tony, Hal, and Trina.

The teddy bear was a hit. Trina especially loved it. I placed it on Aunt Belle's bed with my pocketbook. We settled in for lunch with Ramona in Trina's lap and Randolph sitting on the floor between the two boys. It didn't take long for those cats to figure out from whom they could get tasty treats.

Tomorrow was Sunday. I needed Mrs. Taylor's lock and key. I was bursting to tell everyone about the engagement, but I didn't. It was hard. I managed to keep my mouth shut.

I paid the kids for their work. Trina kept trying to give me money for the bed frame. I finally took a one-dollar bill out of her stack. "Done. Paid for in full. I don't want to hear any more about it."

## CHAPTER 55

William called that night. I was ironing my dress for church. "I picked up the ring. It is beautiful. I think Miss Belle would be pleased. Mr. Taylor cleaned it. You can hardly look at it without sunglasses!"

"What time will you pick me up? It has taken my last reserve not to tell anyone. I can't wait to see you."

"Instead of picking you up, Honey, would you meet me on the front steps of the church at 10:45?"

"Well, yes, I can do that, William. But why? You don't have to work, do you?"

"I need to do a couple of things in the morning. I am afraid I will be running late. This will just make it easier on me." He replied.

He wouldn't tell me much more about his plans, so we agreed to meet as he asked. I finished ironing my dress. My fingernails looked awful. Even with wearing the latex gloves, the work had taken their toll on my hands and nails. I spent the rest of the evening doing my nails and talking to the cats.

"Kitties, William and I need to make a final commitment about moving into Ring-a-ding's. It definitely is a place with a past. Morton's stink comes and goes. I don't think I can sell the house because of Morton. I am not sure I can live in it with Morton. What do the two of you want to do? You are part of the family. You have lived several years in Belle's place. You should have a vote."

"I just wish everything were normal. I love being at Ring-a-ding's. I would really like to move into her house. It is Morton. I am afraid of him.

147

I can't even spend the night over there anymore. Clarisse doesn't scare me. I feel as if I need to be there for her. Morton was or maybe still is messing with her. She said he was touching her."

"Dear Lord, I need some direction and help."

"I know we can do what Belle and Charlie did. We can close Morton's door and seal it off. We know he can come out with the door open. I don't know if he can escape if we nail it shut. We can live in the first floor and maybe in the other three rooms upstairs. Morton sure is a thorn in all this."

"I really do want to live at Belle's place. It is the closest thing I have to a home. My little house is too small. William and I could live happily at Ring-a-ding's. If we have children, it will be the perfect place for our family."

"Do you think I should consult one of those psychics on TV? We would certainly make the show. Two ghosts. One little girl who thinks I am her mama and Morton who thinks I am the enemy. I think Morton might be the devil incarnate."

"So, Kitties, what do you think? Shall we pack up and move back to Belle's place?" When I asked this, both cats crawled into my lap and began purring loudly. Ramona reached up and patted my face. I think I understood their vote was to go back home.

"William is off on Monday. I have been thinking about going to the historical society. I don't know if they have much on Morton or the Purvis family. There may be some newspaper articles on the moonshine industry in town. We have got to get Morton to leave. Surely, there is a way."

# CHAPTER 56

It is six in the morning. I can't sleep. I am too excited.

The cats and I had breakfast. I gave them a whole can of tuna. They will either eat themselves into a stupor or throw it up on the rug. I didn't care. We were celebrating.

I put on my lavender dress with the full skirt. I had brought Uncle Charlie's green hat box home with me. Uncle Charlie's Panama hat with the yellow rose was inside. I put it on my head and looked in the cheval mirror. I put Ring-a-ding's iris broach on the left shoulder of my dress. I was ready for any and everything. I couldn't stay at home. I only hoped I could keep my mouth shut at Sunday School.

I was absolutely giddy.

I had no idea what the Sunday School lesson was about. I'm not sure I even participated in the class. I do remember someone telling me they liked my hat. I told them it was Uncle Charlie's. I do remember explaining how Belle had created it for me. That was all I could recall of the morning.

I walked around from the back of the church to the front. People were visiting with each other during the twenty minutes between church starting and Sunday School ending. It was very common on pretty days for people stand around outside. I was surprised at the size of the group this morning.

I was trying to get to one side of everyone to wait for William. I wasn't in the idle chatter mood this morning. I was afraid I would spring a leak and tell everyone our secret.

"There she is!" Someone yelled.

I looked around. I didn't see anyone or anything to be pointed out.

Oh. OH. They are yelling and pointing at me.

There were balloons tied to the church marquee. Mr. Dewey, the choral director, and two of the high school boys were standing with William. The boys started playing guitars. Mr. Dewey stepped forward.

"The first time ever I saw her face," he sang. William dropped to one knee in front of me.

"Patricia, I fell in love with you the first time I saw you. I have loved you more each day. Please, marry me."

Well, so much for the make-up I had so carefully done that morning. I was squalling. I lunged for him. The two us went tail over tea kettle in the front walk. People were clapping and cheering. Mr. Dewey was still singing. We lay on the ground hugging, laughing, and kissing.

People helped us up. Someone stuck my hat back on my head. William slid Ring-a-ding's ring on my finger. It was blinding. Maybe it was my tears or the sunlight that made it flash. I think Ring-a-ding and Uncle Charlie were shining some happy glow on it.

People were hugging and kissing on us. My head was spinning with congratulations and best wishes.

Church was delayed at least a half hour.

We and most of the congregation went to lunch at the Country Buffet. Bella's ring was googled over time after time. William wanted to make a splash, and he certainly did. We posed for pictures and received so many good wishes.

## CHAPTER 57

We finally made it back to my house. We collapsed on the sofa. Both cats looked at us. Ramona landed in William's lap and Randolph in mine. William was holding my hand. "I'm exhausted. I'm happy, but I am exhausted." I had to agree with him. The adrenaline rush was over. The four of us went to sleep on the couch.

I awoke to the smell of coffee. William's suit coat and tie were laying on the chair. Ramona was curled on top of them. I'm sure she believes everything looks better with cat hair. She was marking William as her daddy.

I walked into the kitchen and found William buried in the refrigerator. "Honey, what you looking for?"

He jumped about two feet in the air. "I was trying not to wake you up. I'm sorry."

"I surely didn't need to sleep my big day away. All that you did, all the people. Well, everything. It was great, but I guess I used up all my energy. I was too pooped to pop when we got home."

William was putting breakfast together. "I'm starving. I don't think I even ate my dinner. If I did, I don't remember it. Do you want pancakes?"

"If you cook it, I will eat it. You know you may have to take over the cooking part of the marriage contract. Cooking is not one of my best talents."

Over coffee and pancakes, we discussed our living options. William agreed as long as Morton was there, we couldn't sell the house. We could live on the first floor, but that seemed so illogical. Here we have a wonderful second floor inhabited by Morton and Clarisse. There had to be a way to reclaim it.

My lease was up in six weeks. I would tell my landlord I would not renew. That gave us six weeks to do what we needed to the first floor of Belle's house. I could move in while Mr. Horace's crew continued to work. I told William I would ask Mr. Horace if he thought the main floor could be finished in six weeks. The first-floor bathroom, the fireplaces, and the kitchen were the three big jobs. I could sleep there at night and stay out of the way during the day.

"I don't know, Patty. I imagine he will want to do the bathrooms at the same time. He is going to tie all the plumbing in somewhere. I imagine it will tie into Belle's bathroom. If not there it will have to connect into the kitchen pipes. I am not sure you can split the jobs as you are talking about. Maybe you should extend your lease for a month. Talk to Horace about the time frame." William suggested.

Feeding bacon to Ramona and Randolph, I asked them if they wanted to go back home. Ramona looked at me and let out a "mik-mik" sound and rubbed against my leg. "I think she is saying yes." said William who now had a lap full of Randolph. "I believe he agrees."

Cleaning up the kitchen together, we talked about what we needed to do. I told him about Christine's house. "I would like to see it. I don't know if we can adapt the back porch as a sunroom. It certainly would be a nice addition."

We continued talking. I told him I would get in touch with Christine so we could visit. We wandered around my little house. I noted the few pieces of furniture I wanted to take. Much of it had come from Belle's place anyway. It should go back home.

After a little canoodling, William went home. The cats and I sat on the sofa. I was making lists of things. I would move Uncle Charlie's bed into Morton's room. I needed to order new mattresses for Belle's bed. The feather mattress was ok, but it needed replacing. In time, I would probably replace all the other mattresses. I hoped Morton wouldn't take over one of the other beds upstairs.

By taking Charlie's bed out, the downstairs room would be huge. On Charlie's side of the room, we could build one long closet. That would give us about twelve feet of closet from the wall to the door. Taking out the fireplace would give another five or six feet from the door to the kitchen wall. We could place a chifforobe or a dresser there.

I was beginning to see possibilities one room at a time. Yes, William and I had made the commitment to move to Belle's place. It just felt right. That night I dreamed of little worker bees and fairies in hard hats.

# CHAPTER 58

William was at the house when I got there. I told him about Belle's room and what I was thinking for a closet. He liked the concept. He called Mr. Horace. William asked if he could come by to discuss some renovations to the house. Mr. Horace said he be there in about an hour.

"Patty, if we can't live upstairs because of Morton, the stink bomb, we can turn Belle's room into the master suite. What do you think about enlarging Belle's bathroom on the back porch side? You could put sliding doors on the closet you want to build. I think you need about five feet for the depth of a closet. Sliding doors would not open into the room, so they would not take up as much space. That is a big room."

The kids came in and started taking all the shelves down in front of the kitchen windows. Trina was definitely the one in charge. I hadn't mentioned the kitchen. She had made her roster of tasks and was pushing the boys on through it.

The kitchen windows really needed it. I don't think they had been cleaned since Daddy put up those shelves.

The smell was faint when William and I wandered upstairs. We looked at Morton's room. "If you take Morton's room for a bathroom and closets, you won't be able to move your Uncle Charlie's bed up here."

I hadn't thought about it. I was just trying to place things I wanted to keep. "Come in the sewing room."

We moved the two farm tables apart. "Let's put this one in front of the window and shove the other one next to it." William began shifting things. "We still have a good five feet open on that wall like this. If we pull this table into the corner, you could put Mr. Charlie's bed where the two tables were. You will still have a workspace, and you can keep his bed. Do you still want to make this an office?"

"You could move one of these tables in front of Clarisse's window. Her bed is smaller." He said as he walked back into her room. "Put a closet in the fireplace. You can have an office in here. Just think about it."

"I know you said you wanted to leave Belle and Charlie's bedroom alone. But, Honey, you could put a closet in their fireplace space. If you moved their bed over to the inside wall, you'd have room for both chifforobes on each side of the window. That way you could leave her old stained-glass lamp in the window."

I told William that I liked his ideas. We moved a few pieces of furniture around. I could see his point. Once the chimney space was turned into closets, we'd be able to keep the old furniture and have more space plus a closet.

"I still think I want to make Aunt Belle's sewing room into an office. Like you said, I can put Uncle Charlie's bed where the two tables were, add a closet, and use the table for a desk. I want to move the old wooden file cabinet in here. Do you want a regular desk, or will you use the other table?"

We were still talking and measuring when Tony called up the steps. "Mr. Horace is here with Mr. Herman. Want me to bring them up?"

Morton's odor was not very bad this morning. The two men came up and congratulated us on our engagement. We walked around the upstairs rooms. William and I explained the need for a second bathroom and closet space.

Mr. Horace had William holding one end of the tape measure as they moved around the different rooms. I asked about converting part of Morton's room into a bathroom. "Let me look at the plumbing and the rooms downstairs. Then we'll see."

He roamed all around the house. I told him about Christine's sunroom, and I wondered if we could do that.

"I built that. My team and I did all the work on her house. Your house is in so much better shape. Her place had bad termite damage. That entire back porch was practically falling off the house. She had wood timbers as underpinning. You have brick. I'll go under the house and check the flooring timbers before I leave."

"Just looking at things here, I think we can do a lot. We could add a sunroom that would take in the whole porch. What I would do is glass in the porch as it is. The whole house probably needs more insulation underneath. We can install more insulation under that porch and the house if it is needed. We could put tile or linoleum on top of the old floor. That would stop any air leaks and keep it a little warmer. We might caulk that porch floor. Leave the floorboards looking like they do right now. Let me look and ponder on it."

He wandered off musing "You could caulk that old porch floor... keep the original wood... move the bathroom wall out about two feet or so. Put a door to the bathroom in the sunroom..."

Mr. Herman and I went to the kitchen for coffee. The kids were working hard on the windows and shelves. Trina sat down with us. Looking at the ring, she said "I can't believe you didn't tell us you were getting engaged."

I confessed it had been a hard secret to keep. She and Mr. Herman were laughing about the scene in front of the church. "Did you know it went viral on Facebook? It was a good thing you were wearing a slip under your dress!"

"Eek!" She showed it to me and Mr. Herman. Mortified was the only word I could think of. My skirt had flounced up in the air, leaving my slip covered bottom exposed to the world. Herman started laughing. "Trina, show me how to find that. How do I send it?"

"Mr. Herman! You wouldn't dare." I pleaded.

"Oh Patty, that is the best thing I've seen in a long time. You didn't show your fanny too badly. Everyone loves it that you two are together. I want to show it to Hazel." Mr. Herman was laughing so much he had tears coming down his face.

I had a sinking feeling everyone at the Masonic Lodge and the Eastern Star would see my fanny.

Tony laughed, "Mama was standing next to Mr. William when you got him. She said you almost took her and three Deacons down with you. Hal said, "If I ever propose to someone, I am doing it when there isn't anyone around."

It was done. I couldn't undo it. I could be embarrassed about it, or I could laugh about it. I had to admit it was rather funny to see.

William and Horace came into the kitchen. I asked if they wanted coffee or a coke. "Can I get a big glass of cold water, Patty? A lot of people don't like to drink plain water, but I do. I drink me almost three gallons a day when I am working in the heat."

"Patty, it looked like Belle took really good care of this place. No termites, no rot, nothing wrong that I can find. You think about that sunroom. Take William and go over to Christine's place. If I were you, I'd just enclose the porch with windows. You don't have to tear it all out. Save you a lot of money and time. And it would look right nice on this old house."

"If you want, we can make the downstairs bathroom bigger. You got good space in there. There is insulation, but if I were you, I would put more under the bathroom and run a good thickness under this porch. Caulk in between the porch boards and leave them like they are. Be pretty with glass and that old floor. The porch doesn't need painting unless you want to change the color." Mr. Horace kept doodling on his pad.

"Now, upstairs is a bit of a different story. I think you got a dead rat in the walls somewhere. I could smell that stink of decay. If we take about half that bedroom, we could make you a good size bathroom with a walk-in shower, or we can put in a tub. Tubs are good if you have little kids. Showers are better when you get old."

Drawing on his yellow pad, he divided Morton's room about halfway. Adding the toilet and sink fixtures, he showed us how to place a tub so we would have a window above the toilet. And then he did an amazing thing. He took the other half of the divided area and wrote "closet."

"This will be a good-sized closet for this upstairs. If you would rather, you could open a door into that bedroom. It could make a small guest bedroom or even an office space. We can take out the fireplace and make this a square room, or you can leave that corner cut like it is and leave the fireplace. If you take out the fireplace, it will give you an addition five and half feet on each wall."

"If it was me, I'd take all the old chimney and fireplaces out. You don't need them for heat, and that old brick and mortar can loosen over time. I am surprised that parts of the chimney haven't crumbled in on itself."

"I'll figure you up some prices and come back on Wednesday if that's ok. We can talk about it all then. You think about that old porch now, ya hear. I really think you should glass it in. Put you a double glass door in the kitchen going out to it. Save your money and put it in the rest of the house."

# CHAPTER 59

I was overwhelmed with all the numbers and information Mr. Horace had given me. William looked even more stunned.

"I crawled under the house with him. There must be three dozen Mason jars under there. I found a skeleton of a cat, too."

I started laughing. "That was Thomas the Tom Cat. He liked being under house. When he got sick and died, Aunt Belle said to leave him. He'd picked out his spot for eternity."

We talked about the sunroom first. We both agreed glassing it in with windows and sliding glass doors would make it useable all year round. I really did like the idea of the double glass door in the kitchen. It would let in lots of light, and I could open it up so the sunroom and kitchen could feel like one big room.

William copied down our sunroom/kitchen ideas. I told him I would like to repaint the kitchen when we do this. I am not 100% sure of the color but something other than what it is now.

"Oh, thank God. I know pink was her favorite color, but this is just awful." William was laughing.

Trina said her class in Home and Life Skills had a chapter on how color affects people. The police use this color in drunk tanks and in insane asylums to calm people down. If you stay in it too long, it will make you hyper. Maybe we knew some the problems of the house now. It was being driven crazy by those awful pink walls.

# CHAPTER 60

We went upstairs. Ramona and Randolph in the lead. "Hey Morton, did you hear? People think you are a dead rat." I laughed.

The stench grew a little in intensity. I stopped laughing.

"Morton, I know you can hear me. I saw you beating the bed. You have the power to move things. Can you write to me? Can you tell me what you need? We have to come to an understanding. William and I are going to live here. I'd rather it be with your blessings than without. Tonight, I am going to leave you a pad and pen. If you can write, do it. If you can talk, speak to me now."

Nothing.

We measured off the future bathroom and closet space. We decided a squared corner in place of the chimney would really be a good thing. I wasn't sure Uncle Charlie's bed would be able to fit in the space left. The big closet might be best. If I had to give up his iron bed, I would reluctantly do so. Maybe I could put it in the new office. I wasn't going to throw anything out until I tried every possibility.

"Miss Patricia? Can we come up?" called Tony.

"Of course, you can. Why couldn't you?" I asked

"Trina said you might be huggin' and kissin' or something up here. We weren't supposed to interrupt anything." Tony looked down at his feet.

"Oh, you three silly geese. Come on up here. We'll show you what Mr. Horace was talking about. I want to hear what you think."

We were all in agreement. I would call Horace that evening and tell him our decisions. That way he only needed to work up prices for this one job. He need not waste his time on the speculation of other options.

"We're done downstairs. Can we go out back to the shed in the back where Morton's old car is?"

"I don't think Morton's car is there. I imagine it has been gone many years. I don't care if you want to go wander around, but that place is a mess. Mr. Otis said the trees and black berry vines had grown up around it. There is probably barbed wire on the ground and still attached to those rotten fence posts. You know there are rattlers and copperheads in those woods. You may go, but you be really careful. Keep your cell phones on. You call if you need us."

We had really become dependent on cell phones. I remember when Uncle Charlie brought home some walkie-talkies. He could talk to Belle in the house. He would go out to the different lots and speak to people working. He was the talk of the town. Uncle Charlie was high-tech! After that, farmers started using walkie-talkies more in the fields.

Uncle Charlie was going to let some men hunt deer on the farm. He told Belle he was going to make them carry a walkie-talkie for safety. She told him he had best be sure those were long range gizmos because they'd be talking to Charlie from Pender's field. Nobody was hunting on their land as long as she was breathing. I think Uncle Charlie knew she would say that. I remember him just laughing and laughing.

Cattle and hogs were grown on this farm. The animals were butchered for food. I never saw any of that. I hated it and so did Belle. Mama grew up on a working farm and was better able to deal with it. Belle and I stayed in the house and pretended none of that was happening.

"We know to be careful. Hal and I have snake boots in the truck. Trina is wearing her cowboy boots. They are almost as good as snake boots. We'll go ahead of her. I promise we'll look out for each other." Tony said as they went down the porch steps.

# CHAPTER 61

"Miss Patricia! Mr. William! Y'all come quick." William jumped off the back porch and was running toward the new barn. Trina was running toward him yelling. I came running behind. I was afraid one of the kids had been bitten by a snake.

William grabbed Trina "What is it? Are you all right? Where are you hurt? Is one of the boys hurt?"

He was screaming at her so fast she couldn't answer. He had picked her up in a hug and was running back toward me.

"STOP! Mr. William. STOP!" Trina was trying to get out of his arms. "I'm not hurt. Nobody is hurt. We found the car."

It didn't register at first. He wouldn't put her down and was still carrying her to me. "I reached them and put my hand on William's arm.

"Tell me again, Trina. Nobody is hurt? The boys are okay?"

"No'm. They're all right. We found the car. We found Morton's car."

William's chest was heaving as he was trying to catch his breath. Supporting his upper body with his hands on his knees, he gasped "Don't...ever...scare me...like that... again."

"I didn't mean to scare you. We were all just so excited. I didn't know you were so strong, Mr. William." She smiled shyly at him.

I thought to myself "Mr. William didn't know he was that strong either. When this fear induced adrenaline fades, William will be flat out exhausted. Every muscle in his body would be sore."

"Show us, Trina."

The old shed was really grown up with trash trees, black berry bushes, and thorny brambles. The boys had used limb loppers to clean a ragged path to the door. I think the old barn door more than likely fell off the rusted hinges. The boys didn't need to pry it open. The brambles were all that was holding the structure up.

Inside sat a black humpbacked car probably from the late-thirties. It looked as if it has just been parked. There really weren't too many vines in the shed. There were old tires and trash in there though. The car's tires were all flat with dry rot. The headliner looked like it had rotted and fallen into strips.

Hal had managed to crawl over all the trash to reach the car. He was working on the driver's side door. He couldn't get it open because of all the junk around it. He managed to pry it open a few inches. It was just enough to look inside. The interior was dusty but looked to be mostly intact. It looked as if field mice may have made a nest in the back seat.

"I wonder how bad the frame is. It might be something you could restore. Hal and I could help you with it. Couldn't we, Hal?" Tony was excited about the relic.

Tony's eyes were wide with desire. He and his daddy had loved working with that old '49 Ford truck. Looking at William, I could see the same expression on his face. I think the three boys, including William, had a project here.

William and Tony had managed to get the hood open. "The wiring is shot, but the engine looks like it is in good shape. We could drag it out with a wrecker. You'd look cool going to school in a Moonshiner's car, Honey."

I thought to myself we have enough projects. If William would like to play with this old car, I didn't care. I thought it looked neat and would be a treat to have it up and running, but first we need the house done. I just had to keep the focus on the house.

William and the boys continued to make plans for Morton's old car. I told Trina to let them get it out of their system. After the house was done, they could play with their new toy all they wanted.

# CHAPTER 62

Tony's daddy called. He had news about the old guns and wanted to talk. I asked them to come on over. Darryl, his brother Tim, and their daddy showed up about thirty minutes later. The kids had waited for them to come. They told them all about the car. Everyone went back to see this marvelous find.

The general consensus was it was a 1938 Ford. Mr. Melvin, Tony's granddaddy, said he remembered the car. "Morton drove it. He always kept it hidden from his folks. Charlie had a Ford pick-up and seems like they had black Ford sedan. I don't rightly remember the sedan. It was just their church car or if Belle had to go some where's."

Mr. Melvin continued with his story "Morton was sneaky. He was good friends with that oldest Purvis boy. They both got into a lot of trouble. I think his name was Joshua or Jonah. I can't rightly remember. He was kilt drag racing. He passed the Burton's boys car and hit a truck loaded with hay head on. Ol' man Brownlee was driving. He was hurt bad. He didn't walk for pert near a year. Then he had a bad limp."

More discussion and plans about the car were going around the kitchen table. Finally, Daryl got back to the guns. Some of them were collectible, and all of them were in great shape.

Those men were like kids about the guns. They had the best time telling us the history and showing us all the features on the guns. They behaved like grown kids with big, dangerous toys.

Each of the guns gleamed. Mr. Melvin had enjoyed cleaning and polishing the weapons. He had an appreciation for the beauty and craftsmanship for them. He had cleaned and waxed all the wood as well. The wooden stocks glowed.

I asked about the hog leg. "I think it was Charlie's gun. Morton may have used it, but if'n you look right 'chere on the butt, you can see CDL. They's Charlie's initials. It could be his paw's. Charlie was a junior named after'n his daddy. That hog leg is old enough to be his paw's gun. I never seen Charlie carry that gun." Mr. Melvin explained. "If'n you want to keep the hog leg, Patty, I think you should. I am almost positive it was Charlie's paw's. I don't think you should worry it was used in a killin'. Well, now, it might've been used in a killin', but probably not anybody kilt by Morton."

I was relieved. I wanted the hog leg. I may not do anything, except display it on Charlie's desk, but it fascinated me for some odd reason. Darryl told me to get a gun permit to carry concealed. He asked to see Charlie's .38 in the dresser drawer.

I brought the pistol out to him. He slid it into a beautiful tooled leather holster and handed it back to me. We all think you should take this with you when you go out. If you stay in the house by yourself, you need to keep it where you can get your hands on it easy."

"You're a young gal, Patty." Mr. Melvin said. "I think you ought to have that pistol on you all the time when you are out here by yourself. Even if William is here, you tote that gun. It won't hurt William none to have a gun, too. Tim, give him that .45 to carry."

"Y'all listen to me. Them coyotes are getting more 'n more bolden. Don't you ever hesitate to shoot at one of 'em. They'd steal your chickens in a blink of an eye. They'd turn on you in a heartbeat. They's mean and powerful."

"You watch your step too out'n the yards, young'un. Now you had them fields cut, them snakes'll be out moving more. They's got to find them new hidey holes. Get you some good work boots, not them tenny shoes." Warned Mr. Melvin.

Tim had done amazing work with the old leather. "This is Grandma's pocketbook. I thought you might like to see it. It was a piece that the leather goods man did. He did the rifle case, too. See, this is his stamp. Here it is on her pocketbook."

"These belts are too big for you like they are. I think this one might have been Charlie's. He was a small man. I punched two more holes in it. I think you can put the holster on it, and it will fit you. I can add more holes, too." Tim was maneuvering the holster onto the belt.

It fit me perfectly. I popped Uncle Charlie's pistol in the holster. I thought I looked like Annie Oakley. Only cuter.

"If'n you want to tote the hog leg, Patty, you got to get a different belt and holster. It's too big for you. Firing that thing will land you flat on your fanny. It kicks almost as bad as a shot gun. I think you should keep it as a memory. Not a totin' weapon. I told Darryl not to put no bullets in it." Mr. Melvin was shaking his finger at me.

I was advised if I wanted to sell any of the guns, I should let Darryl handle everything. He would talk to one of the men with whom they did business. That was a relief. I asked Daryl and Mr. Melvin if they would just handle that for me. They could have a percentage of each sale. I had to convince them they earned a share of the sale. Finally, this was agreeable to everyone.

Mr. Melvin asked me if I cared if he bought the rifle and the leather case. "It was Charlie's. I'd love to have it. Charlie and me growed up together. He was like my bother in a lot of ways. There's another rifle, better'n this 'un, but I'd like to have Charlie's."

"Mr. Melvin, for what you all are doing for me, I want you to have Uncle Charlie's rifle and that beautiful case. You take them home, and you love them."

"I'll sell my old rifle and give you that money."

"No, you won't. Keep that old rifle. Better yet, give it to your grandson. Tony will love it because it was yours. You take Uncle Charlie's and when time comes, you leave Uncle Charlie's to Tony, too. That would make Charlie proud. It makes my heart feel good to know it will be Tony's someday."

Hugs and tears.

William and I went upstairs to find the cats asleep on Clarisse's bed with her doll sitting between them. William moved a little table into Morton's room. I placed a pad and pencil on it. "Morton, if you can, tell me what I can do to help."

# CHAPTER 63

The cats and I got to the house early the next morning. The kitchen looked so bright with the clean windows. I wasn't sure I would put all three of the glass shelves back up. With Mr. Horace glassing in the end wall of the porch, I might just put the shelves in the sunroom. These windows could be left open to look out into what Belle called the side garden. I have a picture of her and Charlie standing in front of the huge bridal wreath bush. I had framed it. It sat on my desk at home.

It was a garden that had gotten overgrown. I needed to spend some time pulling weeds and trimming back shrubbery. There was an old root cellar dug in at the back on the right side. I knew the doors were still there. I didn't know if it would even be safe to go down in the old cellar. I probably needed to have that filled in with dirt.

The outhouse still stood in the very back of this side lot. Looking out these windows in the kitchen I started imagining the flowers back in their glory. The bridal wreath had a few straggly blossoms on it now. After the bloom season, I would cut it back about one-third. A little fertilizer and water would have it showing out next summer. I could see where daffodils and iris had bloomed earlier. With the windows covered and dirty, I hadn't noticed.

I would ask the kids if they could help me clean up the side lot. I was going to repair the old outhouse and leave it standing. It was a neat old building. A two-holer! A deluxe outdoor toilet.

The root cellar doors, outhouse, and other small buildings had been painted barn red. Much of the old paint was faded and gone. Silvery wood was now exposed. The root cellar would be a good place to store garden tools if it were safe. Of course, the outhouse would be good storage, too. Guinea Girl roosted in the old oak that spread its limbs over the outhouse. She was there now.

"Hey Guinea Girl. What are you doing up in that tree at this time of day?" She answered by standing up, flapping her wings, and setting back down to roost.

I went back in the kitchen and looked out the windows again. I would leave them open. I could see Guinea Girl on her perch. The side garden would be a pretty flower bed again. I'd work on it while the men worked inside the house. I'd ask Mr. Horace if he would add a water faucet at that end of the porch, too. I made a note on my pad. My lists were getting longer. I couldn't remember all the things I needed to ask or do. Thank goodness for this pad of memory triggers.

I wasn't expecting the kids today, but they may show up. If they did, they'd probably want to play with the old car. William and Hal had talked about pulling the car up to the stable side of the new barn. There were double doors on each side. It has been designed that way, so a tractor or a wagon could enter from the back lot, close the doors, and exit into the front lot. The car would be out of the weather, and they could work on it all they wanted.

I more or less had a free day to myself. The kids and I had completed pretty much all we could do in the house. I had a good day's worth of work sorting through Aunt Belle's broaches and scarves. I decided to go through the old clothes upstairs and determine if any would be of value. The lady at the historical center told me they wanted some period clothes and items that could be used in the display rooms. What she couldn't use I would offer to Dana for some of her fabric creations.

I had put aside a few books to take to the historical society as well. I found several pair of eyeglasses and one spectacle case. I could give them those. Maybe I would put the case and the really old glasses on Uncle Charlie's desk. With the hog leg. I would soon have that old desk covered in memories.

I could stay busy in the house. I needed to think about the wedding.

William and I had mentioned getting married at Christmas break. We'd have about six months to plan the wedding and work on the house. I didn't know how far Mr. Horace would get in that time, but the downstairs probably would be livable for us.

I was taking a cardboard box upstairs when I heard knocking on the kitchen door. It was Tony. "I haven't swept the yard this week, and I need to get that done. Hal and I want to clean out the stable of the new barn so the car can be moved. That okay with you?"

"If that is what you want to do, it's fine with me. I don't see any need to sweep the yard. Mr. Horace's crew will be in and out. You just be careful out there. At one time there was an electric line run to the old barn, but I think it has been gone for years. You won't have any light. Snakes might be hidden in the dark corners." I was concerned about them.

"We both got our cell phones, and we're wearing our snake boots. I brought Daddy's arc light and Hal's bringing his daddy's big battery-operated light that he puts on their boat when they go fishing. We'll have it lit up really bright. You come see when we get it ready. "

"Where's the third musketeer?" I asked

"She moved her new bed into her room last night. She and her mama are fixing her room and cleaning out closets today. Hal said going through Trina's closet would take a week, not a day. He said she has more shoes than Belk's department store has." Whistling, Tony grabbed up his broom and started sweeping off the porch.

# CHAPTER 64

Typical of the cats. If I set a box down, either Ramona or Randolph was in it. I lifted Ramona out of my box, and we went upstairs. Randolph followed behind us. The smell was very faint today. Oh, I remembered then. I had left Morton a pad of paper so he could hopefully communicate.

The pencil was laying on the floor. The pad was as well. It had something faint drawn on it. Maybe Morton and I were communicating.

"Morton, good morning. I see you left me a message. I am so proud of you for doing this."

I stared at the mostly round like form. It had a head shape—maybe. There was a medium sized lopsided circle and a larger one behind it. There were dots all over the biggest circular shape. I was clueless.

I carried it to the sewing room. I sat in front of the window where I got get the best light. I turned it every direction I could. I placed it on the floor and stood looking down at the lopsided rounded forms and dots. No matter from which direction I looked, I couldn't decipher it.

"Morton, I don't understand your drawing. Can you do more? Can use words or letters?" The smell came back--not as bad or as intense but definitely there.

"Morton, you make that smell when you are displeased or unhappy. Okay, I understand that. You need to know I am trying to help. I don't mean to make you mad. I know tearing up your room did that. Your room was a death hole. I apologize for not talking to you first about cleaning it out, but it had to be done. You need to recognize I am a living being. If I am going to live in the house, we have to have an understanding. Your stink is a big problem."

Suddenly the pad of paper flew across the room. It sailed across the room like a bird in flight. It hit the wall and fell to the floor. The smell began to intensify.

"Okay, Morton, I am going to put the pencil on the table and leave the pad there. Do what you want, but don't throw things at me anymore."

"William, can you talk a minute?" I knew he was at work, but sometimes he caught a break.

"Yeah, what's up?" He asked.

"Would you be able to come to the house when you get off today? Morton drew a picture. I can't make anything out of it, but maybe you can." I told him I thought Morton had thrown the pad in frustration. At first, I thought he was throwing it at me, but now I think he just zinged it off into the air.

"I'll pick up something for supper and be right there. I don't go in until late tomorrow, so I will park behind the new barn if that is okay with you."

"Please. I think we should stay here tonight. With Morton drawing that picture, I think we are at least making some progress. Don't stop for anything. I am going to the grocery store this afternoon. The cats are almost out of their food."

"Clarisse. Morton. I am going to town. Y'all behave and try to write me a note."

## CHAPTER 65

Nothing had changed when I got home. The pad and pencil were still on the table. The cats were asleep with Clarisse's doll.

Mr. Horace dropped by. We finalized our agreement on the changes to the house. His crew would start on the upstairs. "We'll get that dead rat from out of the wall, too. We'll find it, and then the smell will be gone."

UMMMM, I hope so, but I didn't think so.

His men would come in the morning to start taking the chimney bricks out upstairs. He told me to cover everything with sheets. They would put plastic over the fireplace openings and doors. They would run a huge industrial vacuum cleaner to catch a lot of the dust, "but you can't catch it all."

I spent the remainder of the day covering everything with sheets. I tied the sheets around the wardrobes. Then I put plastic sheeting over all the beds. Not thinking, I had covered the upstairs chifforobes. I had forgotten my task with the clothing. Oh well, there was a job for another day.

When William came in, I was working downstairs. He helped me move the furniture and cover it. "This looks like a ghost house in here with all these weird white shapes. Walt Disney would love it." He said.

We ate chicken salad. I had made a green salad with strawberries, almond slivers, and raspberry dressing. The kitties ate their dinner plus dined on chicken picked from the salad. For dessert they tasted their crunchies. I know Aunt Belle fed them well with dry and wet cat food. She told me human food wasn't good for them, but every once in a while, they got a treat. I was pretty sure they got a treat off her plate every night.

I filled William in on the plan with Mr. Horace's men. They would start early in the morning. I wished I had not covered the wardrobe upstairs. I could bring those clothes down and go through everything. William told me he'd help me get them down tomorrow. He had to be a work at 1:00 and would not be through until 9:00 at the earliest. "This might be a good time for you to do some things in the yards. It would keep you out of the house and the noise."

I agreed with him. Maybe Trina would come help me.

Upstairs I showed him Morton's drawing. William took the pad and walked over to the light. "If you hold it this way, these two lines look like legs. I think it is a turkey. Look at this? See that big round thing? That is the tail. This is the head. There are the legs. Doesn't it look like turkey to you?"

"Turkey?" The more I looked at it, the more it did resemble a turkey. Sort of. With a lot of imagination. It could be a turkey. I guess. What does a turkey have to do with Morton?"

"Well, apparently everybody thought he was a mean old turkey." We laughed and went downstairs to ponder the mystery of the turkey.

I told William a few stories about the huge Tom turkey. "I was petrified of that bird. He was enormous and mean. He would chase you out what he considered his territory."

He asked me questions about the turkeys and farm animals. "Oh, could it be a guinea hen? They roosted over the outhouse. No, it couldn't be. Guineas don't have big tail feathers. Maybe the answer is in the outhouse?" I thought aloud.

"I am not sure I want to go out and dig through a hundred years of whatever is buried under the outhouse." William said making a face.

# CHAPTER 66

After another stolen night of love, we woke up to a raining day. We were at breakfast when Mr. Horace knocked on the front door. "Come on in." I yelled.

I met him walking in. "Well, Patty, you did a good job of covering everything. We are covering all the fireplace openings with heavy plastic. That will keep the dust confined as we dismantle them. We'll start upstairs. Where do you want me to stack the bricks? They'd make a pretty patio or a walkway."

We agreed on a place in the side of the front yard to store the bricks. They could take them out the front door and stack them on garden side. They'd be out of the way. I was thinking about using some in the garden as pathways like he had suggested.

"Join us for coffee?" I asked.

"I will, but just for a minute. They'll get the truck unloaded and start taping up the fireplaces. We are going to put plastic on the floors, too. We'll start on the roof. It has finally stopped raining. We'll put a blue tarp on the hole where the chimney came out. I think tomorrow or the next day my roofing guy will come to patch the chimney hole. You won't be able to tell it was a chimney when we get through. On the peak I am going to put a little metal house with a red roof. It will be an air vent for the attic but will look decorative." He showed us a picture of the structure.

"May I have a weathervane on top of it?"

"You can have anything you want. Find you one, and we'll put it on. I got a rooster on mine." Horace laughed.

"We need to see how the chimney looks. Sometimes these old chimneys have a twist in them. You have to follow that twist, so it doesn't collapse on you. Don't worry. We'll get all these bricks gone by the first of next week. If it goes well, we might finish earlier than that."

"After the roof chimney, we'll get all the others in the house down. You still want to leave a false one in the front room? That won't be a problem. You can leave one in the kitchen, too. They back up to each other."

"Jim Fordham is my brick mason. He'll be overseeing the dismantling of the fireplaces. He'll make sure every opening is sealed and insulated. Tom Dempsey and his men will do the carpentry work. While Jim is working on the old chimneys, our plan is to start in the room over the kitchen that you want to put the bathroom in. We'll stud in the wall."

"Patty, we use this really loud vacuum cleaner. While we are upstairs, it probably won't be too bad. When we get downstairs, you don't want to be here. We'll take good care of the house. We'll be real sure everything is locked up tight." I could tell Mr. Horace was going to make this as easy as possible for me.

# CHAPTER 67

William and I brought down Aunt Belles' things from the chifforobe. He wrapped the wardrobe back up. We put everything in the back seat of my car. I could deal with those things at my house while Mr. Horace's' men were working. I would be accomplishing something and still be out of his way. I hoped I might get a little weed pulling done in the side yard while they were working, too.

William left for work. I cleaned up the kitchen and watered all the plants on the porches. They dry out so fast when they are outside in the summer's heat. We had another orchid in bloom. It was sort of an orangey pink. I remember Ring-a-ding seeing it at the Fall Festival. Against all her protests, I bought it for her. She seemed to really enjoy the unusual color. She had put it next to her place on the kitchen table. I was surprised to see it with a flower and some buds so soon.

The big white orchid had five flowers and six buds. It would be pretty for months to come. I thought I would take both blooming orchids home. I would put them on my kitchen table and enjoy them.

I sat down at Charlie's desk. I had laid the hog leg there. I would take that home with me. Having it on the desk or even in the house was too great a temptation for people coming in and out. I had put Ring-a-ding's shot gun and Charlies' pistol in the car already.

The men were finished with covering all the fireplaces. Sitting in the front room, I could hear brick dust and mortar landing on the floor of that hearth. It was a weird noise. It sounded like something scratching inside the fireplace trying to get out.

"Miss Patricia? You in the house?" a man's voice called.

"Yes, I'm here. Do you need me to come up?"

"No'm, I think we found what was causing the smell up here. You got a dead crow in the chimney. I'm coming down to throw it away," yelled one of the men as he descended the steps.

"I hope that is the source of the smell." I said as I looked at the poor bird. He looked awfully dried out. You could see it was kind of mummified.

"So far this is all we found. It's been in there a long time, but it could be what stinks. It doesn't have a smell to it now though." The young man said as he took the corpse outside.

I knew better. That crow hadn't smelled in a long time.

I finished the last thank you note to the generous friends of Aunt Belle's. I had been slowly plugging away at the list over the last few days. Now those were done. I still had a freezer full of casseroles, but everyone was appropriately thanked. Aunt Belle had asked money to be given to the animal shelter, to the church, or to the equine therapy program for special needs children. I wish I knew how much money had come in. I wrote a significant number of notes for flowers as well. I imagined more notices would come in during the next month. At least I was caught up for the moment.

The folder Alfred had given me was still laying there. I had slid all the bank's paperwork in the same folder. I started going through the pages. I found some new file folders. I began dividing the papers into topics and placing them in the indicated folders. It was time I got organized with all the odd notes and pages I had gathered.

I continued to work on sorting the papers and organizing the desk. There was a dictionary dated 1952 in the bottom of the deep desk drawer. I had a flashback of Uncle Charlie. He was holding the dictionary and leaning back in his desk chair. Looking very serious, he would say "Spell encyclopedia" or some other hard word. When I couldn't do it, he would spell it. I repeated every letter. Then he would define it. I would repeat the definition back to him. Then we would spell it again.

Uncle Charlie was the world's best speller. I remember when he got started on crossword puzzles. He and Belle had books of them. She'd ask him to spell a word for her. Uncle Charlie never had to ask for a spelling. Of course, Charlie might have made up the answers to fit the questions. I just know he would tease her with "I got my dictionary. You want it?"

"No, just spell the dang word for me and then get on with your business." She'd huff back.

I had found a few embroidery patterns while going through drawers. I had just stuck them in one of the boxes I had set aside for odd things. Alfred's accordion folder was empty. I flattened out all the patterns. I really needed to iron them and those that I had found in the new barn. I folded the patterns as neatly as I could, placing them in that big folder. I would store them in the sewing room upstairs. I made a note to move Charlie's wooden file cabinet upstairs for things like these patterns and my schoolwork.

I would have liked to have placed some furniture in the sewing room. I was almost positive it was going to be an office space. I didn't know if William would need a desk or if he would want or even could use the second table. We had mentioned using the table, but we needed to talk about what he would need for his office space.

# CHAPTER 68

If we were going to have an office upstairs and use Belle's and Charlie's room for ourselves, I needed to get a phone line up there. There was only one phone in the house. It was a black kitchen wall phone probably from the 1950's. The cord was stretched out and may have been 50 feet long. Ring-a-ding and that phone traveled all through the first floor of the house. Occasionally you'd see her knock over something. "How'd that dang thing get there? It doesn't belong there." She'd huff and puff about it. Then put the "dang thing" back in the same spot, only to knock it off the next time she was wandering around talking on the phone.

I tried to get them to put in more phones. They could leave the old phone in the kitchen. I thought they needed one in the bedroom and in the front room where they watched television. "Nope, don't need no more phones. This one is more trouble than its worth. People always calling with a problem or wanting to sell you something. Nope, I need the exercise from getting up and down to answer the infernal thing." Belle had spoken.

Mama and Daddy finally talked them into having a television. Charlie was fascinated by it. He would watch anything. Belle had her afternoon stories. They only had three channels if you got the antennae right. There was tinfoil on the rabbit ears. Finally, we got cable television. At that time, you had one choice for cable service. As a present to them, I paid that bill every month. Eventually, we had more options. I tried to get Belle to look at another company. She was afraid she'd lose her "stories." Nothing I could say would convince her those shows were available on other service plans. I finally just left her alone. She was happy, and she had her schedule worked out.

I called Belle's cable company and got some prices on increasing the service, adding internet and Wi-Fi to the house. I was blown away by the costs. The phone company had a plan that would install their cable TV and high-speed Internet. That would be combined with the phone bill. It was a tad more than Belle's original service company wanted for a new plan, but it would give me more television channels, better options for the Internet, and more phones.

I told the operator we were remodeling. I asked if we should we wait. We set up an appointment for an installer to evaluate what I wanted and needed. He could plan out the needs of the house. After we had designed a plan, he would set a time to add in his equipment while the house was being done. Good. That was one thing off my to-do. I only had a couple of hundred more to go.

I called my landlord next. I explained I was going to move into Belle's place and would not renew my lease. She told me she thought I would do that. She had heard about "the proposal" as it was being referred to on social media. She wished us well.

The insurance company was my next call. I had all the insurance transferred to my name and my address changed to Belle's place. I would need to change my address on everything. I added that to my to-do list. I'd go by the post office and get those address change cards. I imagined I could change a good many addresses by the phone and internet. Tomorrow I would just deal with that from home where I had internet access. Mr. Horace said they'd be on the first floor working first thing in the morning. The upstairs chimneys would all be down. I needed to be away from the house tomorrow afternoon.

Earlier, I had called Mr. Horace to ask if we could keep a false fireplace in the front room. That was a pretty mantel. I just thought it would look better with the fireplace. "Sure, you can. That'd be great. I'll have them take the mantel out on the front porch. You can paint it or strip it. We can set it right back in place. Think about leaving that one in the kitchen, too."

# CHAPTER 69

Mr. Horace dropped by to check on things. "Patty, let's go upstairs and see how things are going." It was startling. You could see light coming from what once was the fireplace face. Then it was dark.

"What happened?" I asked.

"They're pulling the blue tarp over the chimney hole. Tomorrow it will be sealed up and look like nothing ever happened. If it rains, that tarp will keep the water out. If any birds get curious, they won't get in either." He laughed. "I heard they found a dead crow. Maybe the smell will start to fade. I never heard of an animal that long dead smelling, but you never know what can happen."

One of the workmen handed Horace a small tin box. "We found that wedged up in the chimney shoulder." Horace opened it. There were seven old silver dollars, Morton's missing notebook, and a $5.00 gold piece.

We went back downstairs to find two men cleaning out the fireplace openings. They were picking up bricks that had fallen from above. They swept the dust and debris into a flat face shovel and dumped it into a trash can with rollers. No mess at all was left. "I'm leaving the chimney base under the house. It is a support and won't hurt anything. We're going to match some old pine boards to the floors. You won't really see much of a difference between the new flooring we place and what was originally there. I don't think the old floors will need to be refinished. I knew there was a reason I saved all those old boards from Christine's house. Yep. Waste not, want not."

Mr. Horace and I each took a Coca-Cola to the back porch. We rocked and talked. I told him I wanted to put shelves up for Belle's flowers if I could. We discussed possibilities. He made a couple of suggestions that included putting double doors going out into the yard. "That way you can make the backyard feel like it is part of the inside. Use tall windows for the rest of the walls. Sliding glass doors are not as tight as a window, and you won't be opening them all that much."

I mentioned the old garden and outhouse. I was going to start cleaning that space. It would be nice to restore the old flowers beds. I wanted to use the little space Belle had grown tomatoes again. Mr. Horace said he would put water faucets on both ends of the back porch.

"Those old chimney bricks can't be used to build a house or anything. They have become brittle from all the heat they've had over the years. Think about making a path to the outhouse and up to the cold cellar. There's plenty of them, and if you want more, I can bring you some. After your place, we are going to tear down what's left of the Simpson's place. The fire didn't leave much more than the old bricks and some pipes. They want to build back on the lot. They don't want the old bricks, so you can have them all."

We walked out to the outhouse. He looked in. "You need to reinforce the floor here. Don't you put any weight on it. I'd be afraid it'd give way. The building is in pretty good shape to be as old as it is though. I think it'd be a cute accent to your flower bed. Belle always had pretty flowers. My wife has some that Belle gave her probably 25 years ago."

"Now these old doors going down in the ground are old, old, old. I got some odd pieces of treated lumber left from a job we did building a deck. Let me see it we can't put those old doors on a new wood frame. If'n we can do what I think, you can leave those old cellar doors for another hundred years. They look good there. They look like they belong there. Be a shame to throw them away."

"You know why this is called a root cellar or a cold cellar? Some people call them cyclone shelters because people would hide in them when the tornadoes and bad storms came through. People dug these storage places under and between tree roots a lot of times. Whatever was stored in here was kept cool by the earth and the shade of the tree. My folks had one. When my brother Earl was learning to drive, he drove off into the root cellar. Ma made him get the horse and pull the car out. Then she made him fill in the old cellar in one shovel full of dirt at a time." Horace threw back his head and laughed.

Mr. Horace pulled the doors open and inside the dirt room were...old Mason jars.

"Mr. Horace, I bet there are 150 old Mason jars around here. Do you know anyone that would want them? If they were cleaned, couldn't they be used in canning again? I guess I could take them to a recycling center, but I'd rather give them to people who could use them."

"Patty, go get me some boxes. We'll load these things up. They need to be cleaned. You have to sterilize them before you store food in them. You can buy new lids and rings at the grocery store. My ma used paraffin to seal the jars instead of the lids. You ought to keep a couple of these with the latching glass lids. They are old. They'd look pretty with marbles and buttons in them. The blue ones are usually the oldest. A lot of these with glass lids are Ball canning jars."

We emptied out the root cellar. I grabbed another box and collected all I could reach in the crib. I found some blue jars with Ball on them as well as the Mason jars with the metal frame and glass tops. Some didn't have any names. I put the ones with the glass lids in one box and left them in the crib. I thought maybe I would use them for something. I knew I was not going to do any canning!

The others I gave to Mr. Horace. He said he'd drop them off at the church kitchen. They could run them through the industrial dishwasher. The church ladies would take care of everything and make them available to people who could use the jars. "There's still a lot of people who put up their summer vegetables and make jelly, too. These old jars will be put to good use."

## CHAPTER 70

I rounded up the chickens and said goodnight to Guinea Girl. The cats and I went back to town. I had dust bunnies and those fluffy, webby "goosal" feathers in my hair from the root cellar and the crib. Matching me step for step, the cats and I carried all the clothes inside and dropped them on the couch. Ramona immediately landed on top of them.

"I am nasty, Young'uns. Just plain nasty. I am taking a bath. Then we'll eat." I showered and changed into comfy clothes. I hadn't checked the answering machine in a couple of days. Sale pitches and a few congratulations. Thank goodness, nothing earth shattering had happened.

William called when he got home. We discussed our day. I told him Mr. Horace had gotten all the chimney brick down from the roof and upstairs. He said they would use that big vacuum throughout the house to suck up the brick dust. By tomorrow night the chimneys would be gone. I told him about the boards he had saved from Christine's place and how he was going to splice them in where the chimneys were. William was suitably impressed. "Horace is the ultimate recycler!" he laughed.

I would run by Belles' place first thing in the morning. My plans for the rest of day were to handle everything I could on the internet and phone about address changes. I really needed to get caught up on my email, too. I had to think about packing my place up. I wanted to be fully moved when my lease was up.

"Honey, would you do me a favor tomorrow? How about looking at the calendar and do some wedding planning?"

"Oh, I guess it had slipped my mind." I said. Who in their right mind forgets to plan her wedding?

William laughed. "Look around your winter break from school. I can take time off then. I was looking at Saturday, December 13. Are you superstitious about the number thirteen?"

"I don't think I am superstitious about anything. Thirteen is as good a number as any. That would be a good Saturday." I said, looking at my calendar. "I would be happy to go to the courthouse next week and get married if you wanted to."

"I think after 'the proposal', we had best get married in the church. The town's people might lynch us if we deprived them of a party.

"I guess I owe Aunt Belle a wedding." We agreed to shoot for December 13. He and I would both start making lists of wedding related things that needed to be done. We each needed to create an invitation list. Lord help us if we left anyone off. Maybe I would just put a note in the newspaper to invite everyone.

The cats and I were sitting at the table when the phone rang. It was William's mother. Other than the call he made to her to tell her about the engagement, I hadn't talked with her.

"Patricia, this is William's mother Claire. He called last night. He said you have decided on a date if you can get the church. I am here to help you with anything you want or need. I am not going to be a pushy mother-in law, but I am here. You don't have anyone to help you. Let me do anything I can for you. We are just delighted that you will be part of our family."

The thought of her ending that statement with "you poor little orphan girl, you" went through my head.

I'd met William's family twice. His sisters were delightful. William and his brother could have been twins. I only saw a good-natured family but as in-laws? I hope the good-natured family wasn't an act.

I thanked her. She gave me her email and those of both of her daughters. "You let me know what you need. We will be there for you. We're so excited. We think William has made a good choice with you. Let us help with anything at all."

Shortly after, his two sisters called. Did you get the church? What colors? What kind of dress will you wear? What about flowers? Who would be bridesmaids? My head was spinning.

The church was free, so I reserved it for December 13. The rehearsal would be on the 12th. Did I want to have the reception at the church? What about the rehearsal dinner?

Yikes. Eloping to the Justice of the Peace was looking better and better right now. I did need help. I started making notes.

Then I called my best friend Pickle. Yep, she had been at church and had seen my drawers when I jumped William. Had I not seen her posts on Facebook? Oh, dear.

I explained we would be moving into Belle's place. I would need help with the wedding. She agreed to be my Matron of Honor. "Let William's family handle the rehearsal dinner. That is part of their job. Give his mama as much as you can. My mama will do the bridesmaid luncheon. You got time. Start panicking around October. I'll get out all my notes from my wedding. We can do this, Puddin'."

That was us—Puddin' and Pickle. I felt as if this was going to be okay.

I called William at work. "We've got the date at the church. Your mama called and has offered to help. Pickle is the Matron of Honor. She is totally in control. She has given me a list of things to start thinking about. Sure you don't want to elope?"

I got a lot of things done, including cleaning up the house. I had been doing laundry regularly at Belle's, but it has stacked up here. I was feeling more as if I was back in control things.

# CHAPTER 71

William stopped on his way to work. He had the late shift again. Over coffee, we looked at the to-do lists. He added a few things to his pad and marked them off mine.

"One of the men found Morton's notebook and some silver dollars in this tin. Morton had put it in his chimney. Take it with you and look it over when you can. I think it is a list of Morton's whiskey deliveries and the amount paid. I was hoping it would be something wonderful, but I don't believe it is anything of value.

"Did you check Morton's pad? Did he leave us a note?"

"No, I forgot. With all the people in the house I just didn't think about it yesterday. I will when I go over today."

"William, look at this dress. Do you like it?"

The dress was an ivory color. It had been wrapped in paper and rolled into a pillowcase. It had a sweetheart shaped neckline. Lace spilled over the bodice. The sleeves were gathered above the wrists. The lace at the sleeves was really long, and I thought it probably covered the hands. The skirt flowed from an empire waist. There was a pink sash and a pair of opera length gloves wrapped inside the dress.

"That's pretty. Whose is it? Ring-a-ding's?"

"I think it was Belle's. It wasn't hanging with her other clothes. It looks too big for Aunt Belle, but then she wasn't always so bent and tiny. I don't think it was a wedding dress. It could have been. If it can be made to fit me, would it be alright with you if I wore it to the wedding?"

William hugged me tight. "You wear whatever you want. I think Belle would be tickled pink if you wore her dress. Of course, Mama may never forgive you for not letting her go shopping for a wedding gown with you."

"Pickle might be a little ticked off, too." I smiled.

Miss Martha Kate could make anything. All she had to do was see a dress, and she could recreate it. I called her about the gown I had found. She asked me to bring it by.

She laid the dress out on her worktable. She touched every seam. You are taller than Miss Belle. On her this dress would have dragged the floor. You see how this is longer in the back? It was made to be a train behind her. If I cut about three inches off the length, it will hang tea length on you. I can take the extra fabric and make the bodice larger. The waist will need to be bigger, too. Let's get you measured."

I stripped down to my "necessaries" as Belle called underwear. Miss Martha Kate measured and scribbled notes on her pad. She asked me what kind of shoes I would wear. I didn't have a clue. "You go to town and get you some ivory heels that are no more than two inches high. You can dance in two-inch heels. William is a lot taller than you, but you need comfortable shoes. When you get your shoes, we'll measure you again for the length. You leave me the dress. It is raw silk. It's not as fragile as I would have thought for its age. Belle must have kept it in the dark."

"I need to take the lace off to clean this silk. The lace has some stains. I can get that out. The lace at the bodice will not be quite as full. I'll spread it out to handle your bigger bosom."

Then I was out the door. I had a wedding date, a wedding dress, and a Matron of Honor.

I called Pickle with the news. "That's great. What colors are you using? How many bridesmaids are you having? I am not wearing sequins, and I get to pick out MY dress."

"Uh. No, you will not have to wear sequins. Yes, you can choose your dress. You are my bridesmaid. Do I need more? The dress has a pink sash. I like lavender and yellow. I am in deep doo-doo with this wedding, Pickle."

"Nah, Puddin'. It will be ok. Find out if William's sisters want to be in the wedding. If they do, you really have to use them. Is there any other female that you would especially like to have in the wedding? If so, use her. Then that is all. That would give you four attendants. You don't want more than that. If you can get by with less, do."

"Choose one color. It is Christmas time. The church always has that big tree decorated with gold and white ornaments. Think about red or wine or burgundy. No green. You look awful in green. Send me a picture of your dress. Get your shoes next week if you can."

"Do that and then call me, Puddin'. That is all you have to worry about right now."

I hung up and took a deep breath. I was glad she was so calm about everything.

# Chapter 72

There was a lot of activity. I could hear hammering and sawing. Mr. Horace's truck was parked beside the house. The roof's blue tarp shown against the red metal. It was quite pretty.

The fireplace downstairs had the plastic covering removed. I went up the steps and found Mr. Horace in Morton's room. They were easing a board into the floor of the fireplace.

"We'd got the supports in the fireplace floors this morning. Now all we have to do is cover them with these matching pine boards. We are trying this one for fit and color match. If we have to cut one to be narrow or an odd shape, it will be in the corner. We can cover a lot of the misfits with the baseboard. You'll never know there was a splice here. This man is my best carpenter. He'll be doing all the work on the framing, too." Mr. Horace prattled on bragging on his work crew.

You could tell the men were soaking up Horace's praises. There were smiles all around. "You stay away from the fireplaces, Patty. We are going to get all the flooring in these upstairs today. I hope we can get a good bit done downstairs, too. We won't have to do a lot of shoring up downstairs because the chimney base is still in place. I got a man coming to put insulation under the back porch and bathroom. If there isn't good insulation under the rest of the house, you want me to add it in?"

I told him I trusted his judgement. Anywhere he thought insulation was needed, please add it. I asked him to let me know of anything else he thought might need to be done.

"You ever been in the attic of this house, Patty?"

I didn't' know there was one.

"You come on with me. You be careful. The attic isn't floored. It is just beams. Insulation is laid between them. If you step off, you might go through the ceiling." He led me through a small opening in Belle's and Charlie's room. Uncle Charlie's wardrobe had sat under it. I guess I had never bothered to look up.

Between the joists was laid pink fiberglass insulation. "I think this was done when she had heating and air conditioning put in."

"I am almost positive it was the Briscoe Brothers who did the heat and A/C." I told him.

"That'd be my bet. I am going to get one of the boys to take out that round vent over there. You see it? I think squirrels have been in here. We are going to pull all the vents and put in heavy gage wire and secure the vents back in place. This way the squirrels can't gnaw through it. That okay with you, Patty? An old squirrel nest may be part of that smell you got. I was hoping that dead bird was it, but it's still there. It was mighty strong this morning."

"Yes, Sir. Whatever you see that needs doing, please take care of it. I trust you."

"Now, Patty, I want you to know that your Aunt Belle and Uncle Charlie were good to my family. My daddy worked for Mr. Charlie and others. He was a farrier and black smith. He'd come out to the farms and shoe the horses. Most farriers made you bring the livestock in. When daddy got the pneumonia and couldn't work for a couple of months, Charlie and Belle would come to the house. They'd bring food. They bought shoes and clothes for me and my sisters, so we could go to school. They sent flour and meal to the house. Mr. Charlie had a whole hog that had been dressed and smoked sent to us. I owe them an awful lot. I am not trying to do things to the house that isn't needed. I'll be honest with you. If I could do it all for free, I would."

With tears, I hugged Mr. Horace. "They were the best people in the world. I miss them so much, Mr. Horace. Don't you worry about your

A PLACE WITH A PAST

bill. I know you will be fair, but don't you cut yourself short. You have to earn a living, and you have men to pay. I know you're taking care of me as they'd want you to do. I will be forever grateful."

That sentiment was what I heard from everyone. Belle and Charlie were generous to all. They helped everyone they learned was in need. People are trying to return those favors to me.

I wish Ring-a-ding was with me. Maybe she could talk to Morton and help Clarisse. I wonder why she and Uncle Charlie are not here and the children are?

# CHAPTER 73

I had gone to the bathroom. When I came out, there was a big burly man standing at the door. "Can I help you?" I asked wide-eyed.

"No, Ma'am, I didn't mean to scare you. I didn't know you were in there. I was going to check all the plumbing fixtures and the pipes. We are planning to run the drainage and water from the kitchen, but I wanted to be sure all this was okay. If it ain't, now's the time to fix it. Horace wants me to check to see if this might be a better direction to run the upstairs waste and water. I won't be long."

I got out the vacuum cleaner and ran it along the pathways the men were using. Considering all they were doing the floors weren't very dirty. Some sawdust and brick dust were getting on the floors. A little sweep-up every afternoon won't hurt. Trina was probably right. I got a head of myself. I should have left the cleaning until this was all over.

I had left the cats in town today. I kept looking for them though. I got a Coke and went outside. There were two young men at the root cellar. They had both old doors off the frame and laying in the dirt.

"Hey, y'all. What're you doing? You want a Coca-Cola?"

"Miss Patricia, it's me — Walter." Walter was one of my former students. He and his friend were framing up the root cellar opening.

"What are you doing here, Walter? I thought you went on to college. Are you taking the summer off?" I asked.

They came up on the porch and got a Coke each. "I'm working for the summer to make some extra money. I'll be a sophomore in the fall. Mr. Horace took me on to do odd jobs. I hauled bricks out of the house all day yesterday. He won't let me do anything that I can mess up. This is my friend Toby."

Horace had put them to work fixing the storage cellar doors. After that, they were going to replace the outhouse floor and repair anything else that needed to be done to it. No, there wasn't much of anything they could damage out here, except for themselves.

The chickens and Guinea Girl were not at all happy about the disturbances. No one was laying. They were all staying pretty close to their condominium. Even Guinea Girl was staying with the chickens. She didn't usually associate with them. Zsa-Zsa, who considered herself the Queen Mum of the chicken coup and Guinea Girl were not the best of friends. Zsa-Zsa was very jealous. Guinea Girl thought she was the reigning queen of the whole yard. Therefore, Zsa-Zsa and the other chickens were beneath her. The battle over royalty had ceased for a few days.

Tony, Hal, and Trina came around the side of the house. "Hey, Miss Patricia, come to the new barn with us. We've been working on it.'

We visited as we went to the barn. Trina pulled out her phone and showed me her bedroom. It looked great. She was really proud of her closet. "I took out everything that didn't fit. If I hadn't worn it in the last year, I took it out. Mama cleaned out her closet, too. Tomorrow Mama and I are taking it all to Sheila's Consignment shop. Mama said whatever we made would be mine for new things for school."

The kids had cleaned out all the junk that had accumulated in the stable. They were removing the stall dividers, so they had one large space. The ground was dry and powdery. If they raked it, they'd have a good place to work. I bragged on all they had accomplished and how well everything looked. They beamed.

"Tony, let's talk to Mr. Horace about running electricity out to the new barn. I'd like to have lights on the outside. If Big Foot decides to visit, I want to see him first. I imagine we can put in some florescent lights in the stable. We probably should add lights to the top and bottom floors of the barn."

"By the way, Miss Patricia, tell Mr. William he can park in the stable side of the barn now. He doesn't have to park behind it anymore."

Caught. I know my face flamed red. I couldn't make eye contact with any of them, but I could tell they were looking at me. I think I heard a snicker.

# CHAPTER 74

"Can you run an electric line to the old barn? I'd like to have motion lights on it and some lights inside." I asked Mr. Horace.

"Sure. Tony's daddy does all my electrical work. I'll add it to his list. That smell is back. I just don't know where it is coming from. When we lay the insulation over the chimney space, I'll have one of the men look around up there. You don't smell it in the attic though. It is only in that one room."

I didn't dare tell him what it was. I didn't want everyone heading for the hills because they were working in a ghost's room. A ghost with BAD halitosis. "It's been like this for years. I guess Belle got used to it. Maybe it will all go away one day." I lied. As far as I knew the odor had not existed until I opened Morton's room.

The kids went back to complete the demolition of the stable dividers. It was going to make space for at least two cars. Hal was talking about using the wood they had pulled down to make a tool bench. I thought that was pretty ingenious. I told them to let me know if they needed to buy anything for the project.

They were having the best time planning for Morton's car. Trina wanted it painted purple. The boys were wanting black. We'll see who wins. I was partial to purple, too.

# CHAPTER 75

Pickle called and wanted to know if I had my shoes? What my color selection was and how many attendants. Sigh. I will make decisions today. I promised.

William called. We agreed to meet for his dinner break. I told him dinner had to be all about the wedding.

I ran home and shaved, showered, and shampooed. The cats were under my feet until I fed them. I was racing around the house grabbing what I needed. I had spent too much time at Belle's place. William only had an hour break. I couldn't be late. We had too much to discuss.

I couldn't find my tote bag. Dang it. I carry everything I need in that bag. Grabbing my purse, 3x5 cards, calendar, and a notebook, I shoved it all into a Piggly-Wiggly bag and ran for the car.

He was seated at a back booth at the Waffle House when I flew in through the door. The waitress was bringing our coffee. I do tend to live on coffee.

"William, I have got to get a handle on this wedding thing. We have the date. We have the church. Pickle continues to ask me for more information. I haven't got it." I felt a tear begin to form.

"You are the most organized person I know. Where is your list? I know you have a list."

I laid my notebook on the table, placing the calendar next to it. "William, how many people do you want to be your attendants? Do you care about the colors? We have to choose the cake? Two cakes. You get one and then there is the big wedding cake. Why do we need two cakes? And flowers?

Can we, please, just elope?"

"Stop. Breathe. I think this is all getting to you because you are trying to deal with the house, Morton, and Clarisse. You haven't taken the time to grieve Belle. All the stuff in the house has caused your memories to come to the surface. I think you are trying to mourn over your parents, Charlie, and Belle. Morton is just the cherry on top of the whole mess. You shouldn't have tried to do everything in the house right away. It has been too much for you, Honey."

"If you want, we can put the wedding off until next summer. Don't drive yourself crazy over this. If Belle were alive, she'd be overseeing so much of everything. She isn't here though, so you feel all the burden is on you." William was the sensible one at the table.

"I can take tomorrow off. I am owed a good bit of time because I was covering for Marcia while she was out on maternity leave. Let me take the next two days off. Do you want me to come to your house in town or go to Belle's place?"

I felt my shoulders drop back down into place. They must have been hitched to my ears. He was right. I hadn't had time to stop and recover from Belle's sickness and death. I shouldn't have tried to get the old house ready to sell. There had not really been a rush. I could have worked on it while I was teaching. I had more than enough money to quit my teaching job. I didn't think I wanted to stop teaching though. I loved my job and my kids. I wanted to keep working.

I had jumped in and started on everything at once. That is just what I do. I put all I can think of on a list. Then I attack everything at once. I should have taken the entire summer to tend to Belle's affairs. I needed to step back and prioritize.

We had dinner. Tomorrow, he'd come over, and we'd go to the mall. I would find shoes. He said he needed to buy some things, so we'd make a day of shopping. We'd get everything on the wedding worked out.

Deep breath. Okay, I can do this now. WE can do this now.

# CHAPTER 76

The next morning, we left for the mall. As we drove, we talked through my ever-growing list and my ever-enlarging anxiety.

"Colors. If the dress can be made to fit me, it will be off white silk. There is a pink ribbon that ties into a bow at the back of the dress. Since the church will be decorated for Christmas, Pickle suggested I use white, red and gold for everything. What do you think?"

"That makes sense to me. They have that huge tree decorated in white and gold. Don't they have white and red poinsettias in the windows and at the doors?" William asked.

"Oh, they do. I had forgotten about that. I would need a centerpiece for the altar. I would have flowers to carry. Pickle would have flowers, too. If I did a cranberry red sash and some matching flowers with white roses, maybe I could be done with that. Pickle probably won't let me, but I think that is about all I will need for the decorations. I'd like a deep cranberry red and white rose bouquet. You could wear a red rose with some white baby's breath. Who will be your attendants?"

"I think mine are the Best Man and ushers. I thought I'd ask my dad to stand up with me. Other than Pickle, who will stand with you?"

"I guess I could ask some friends, but Pickle is really the only person who is a close friend. All the others and I have drifted apart."

"That's settled then. Neither of us want a huge wedding. Pickle, Mom, and my sisters want the big wedding! Let's just have two people stand with us. You don't have any family to quote give you away unquote. Dad will be pleased to be my best man. The rest of the family will be happy that I chose him. That part is done. Cranberry, two attendants, red and white roses. Dad and I will wear black tuxedos. You will wear Belle's gown with a cranberry red sash. Let Pickle find something she likes. Done?"

"Okay, then. Wow. What a load lifted off me. I feel like we just made huge progress. Today, I will find shoes. That is the next big thing to get out of the way. Once I have the shoes, I will go see Miss Martha Kate. Alterations can start then. She can do the fittings and work her magic. I'll call Pickle. I know she has ten more things for me to do. I am coping now. Deep breath. We can get this done together. Thank you, William, for being the voice of reason."

William took my hand and kissed it. "Is the big stuff for the wedding out of the way?"

"I don't think so. Pickle was rambling about invitations and the reception. Think we could just feed them cake in the church basement?" I said hopefully.

"Probably not. Between Pickle and my mom, I imagine we'll have a big reception. They'll have the entire town invited."

"All the weddings I remember were in the church basement. There was cake and nuts. There was always some kind ginger ale and sherbet punch. And maybe little sandwiches? The punch would make your mouth pucker after you ate the cake." William made a funny puckering face.

"Mom is planning an outrageous rehearsal dinner. How about I turn her loose on the reception. She, my sisters, and Pickle can do whatever they want. They will be in hog heaven, and we can just show up."

"It sounds perfect. Let's set your mama and sisters up with Pickle for this weekend. After that, we will just let them have a great time making the wedding of THEIR dreams!"

I gave William the index cards with instructions to make one card per person/family he wanted to invite. He was to include all the names and the complete addresses. This would be our invitation list.

"I'll give these to Mom. She already has started a list. I have a couple of friends from college I want to invite. That's it. Mom plans to invite our whole hometown."

# CHAPTER 77

I found my shoes. William got everything he needed. We looked at dresses, but I still preferred Belle's if it would fit.

We ate lupper, a late lunch-early supper, at a place near the mall. It was nice not to have people come up and speak to us. I guess that was ugly, but we actually ate while our food was still hot.

We talked about some more plans concerning the wedding. We set up for Pickle and his family to meet in a couple of days. We'd meet at the church, have lunch, and discuss things.

On the way home, we stopped at Miss Martha Kate's house. She made me try on the dress with the shoes. She did some marking and pinning. She decided the dress would be perfect as tea length. I told her about the sash and the colors. She opened a bin that contained rolls of ribbons in every color and width. There it was—cranberry silk. The dress was tight. I could breathe shallowly, but I didn't think I could get through the entire wedding on one breath.

"I can take three inches off the hem. The dress will be tea length. It will glide around you as you walk. You will wear ivory stockings. The material from the hem will be used to widen the waist and the bosom. You aren't fat; you are just a bigger girl than Belle. She was small all her life. I think this dress is probably from when she was a teenager."

She tied the red ribbon around the dress's waist. With the cascading lace and the red sash—it was perfect.

I removed the dress. Miss Martha Kate did some more pinning and marking. She told me to go home. "Look in Belle's broach box. She had some pieces in that cranberry red color. Find all you can and bring all of them to me. You need something old, something new, something borrowed, and something blue. Old is the dress; new are the shoes. I have the hat, not a veil for you. That is the borrowed. I always sew a little blue thread in my wedding gowns. We have everything covered." Miss Martha Kate smiled. "I'll have the hat ready when you come next time."

We stopped at Dairy Queen. It must have been vintage car night. A lot of people have redone old cars. There were about fifteen in the parking lot across from the Dairy Queen and several more in its lot. William and I visited with the owners admired their cars. William started telling them about Morton's old car.

The vintage car enthusiasts were all excited about it. William explained the car was still buried in the old shed. Several of the men offered to come help. One man offered his wrecker. When the time was ready, he'd pull the car up to the new barn.

# CHAPTER 78

William and I went back by my house and picked up the cats. Ramona ran to William who scooped her up. She liked to ride stretched over one shoulder. She assumed her place and looked down at Randolph and me.

"My princess," laughed William.

"I guess that makes you my Prince Charming, Randolph." He purred and continued to wrap himself around my legs.

I gathered up some things for tomorrow while William played with the cats and their feather boa. I need to buy another one. This one was really straggly. I had pink feathers all over my house.

Once I had everything, we left for Belle's place for the night. I took my car and Randolph. Ramona rode on William's shoulder in his car. He parked in the new barn's stable. They shooed the chickens into their roost and came in through the kitchen door. William was talking to Guinea Girl. She had come up on the porch. I handed him a slice of bread, and he fed her a few pieces.

I had fixed the cat's supper, placing their dishes in front of the old cast iron stove. They gobbled it all up as if they hadn't just eaten a bunch of crunchies at the house in town.

William and I took glasses of sweet iced tea out to the back porch. He was looking at the marks made to enlarge the bathroom. "Since you are going to close this room in with glass, I have an idea about the bathroom. Do you remember that big stained-glass window at Keith's antique shop? The one that had the pinks and peachy colors that you liked so much? I think you should put it in the bathroom. It isn't dark. It has pretty colors.

No one could see in. You would still get a lot of light. And you could stop talking about how much you love it and wish you had a place for it."

I liked the idea. He said he would try to stop by for the measurements to give Mr. Horace. I told him I would call Keith and save William a trip.

We rocked and talked about the remodeling. I told him Mr. Horace said we probably won't need to refinish the floors. The repairs to the chimney space seemed to be matching really well.

"How's Morton's B.O.? Any of the workers passed out from the stink?'

I laughed. "Not that I know of, but Mr. Horace is now convinced squirrels are in the attic, and they are causing the smell. The stretch is there. I hear some of the men talk about it. Sometimes it is really bad, but other times it is faint. Come see what Walter and his friend Toby have done to the root cellar."

We wandered about the side garden. The doors were back in place over the old root cellar. They were still in the old red barn paint, but they looked as if they had polyurethane or a preservative on them. I supposed that would protect the remaining wood from the weather. William opened the doors. The framework and backing were made of treated lumber. These doors would last forever.

We stopped at the outhouse. Guinea Girl flew up to her perch in the old oak. I opened the door, and there was no floor. "I guess the boys have started on this project." I told William what Walter said about Mr. Horace keeping them on jobs they couldn't mess up.

"Patty, I want to go upstairs. Do you think we can get up there with all the work going on?" asked William. "I wonder if Morton had written anything else on the pad. Do you think Clarisse might have drawn the picture instead of Morton? That turkey thing looks more like something a child would draw."

I hadn't thought about Clarisse having created the drawing. "It could be Clarisse. I have a few colored pencils in my tote bag. I can put them and a drawing pad in her bedroom. Maybe she would enjoy them and tell us something." I commented to William. "Let me get my tote bag."

# CHAPTER 79

I went out the car, but the bag wasn't behind the driver's seat where I usually tossed it when I got in the car. Then I realized I hadn't seen it in several days.

"William, I don't know where I left my tote bag. It isn't in the car. I remember having it —when? OH, at the bank. Oh yeah! I put the stuff from Ring-a-ding's safety deposit box in my tote."

"Then where did you put your bag? You don't know, do you?" he laughed.

I had to admit I didn't exactly remember where I had placed it. I was sure I had brought it in with me when I came back to Belle's place.

"I know. I stuffed it in the chifforobe in the back bedroom. I was trying to get it out of sight while people were coming and going. I also got it out of mind. You'll have to help me move both beds to get to the chifforobe. Then we need to take the dust sheets off it."

"Clarisse has been without crayons for years. She can do without them another night. Come on. Let's go see what things are like upstairs. Tonight, when we clean off the bed, maybe I can unearth the wardrobe."

Ah, the smell of Morton was in the air. It wasn't strong when we went upstairs. Entering his room released a stronger scent. The floor where the chimney had been looked great. They had managed to dovetail new wood into old. It was perfect. There were some light lines where the saw had trimmed the wood to fit, but the rest was perfect."

"I think a stain will cover these pale marks on the floor. Horace probably has it all worked out. Just look at this joinery in the walls. If it weren't for color, you couldn't tell where the old wall ended and the new started. This old bead board must be something that Horace had salvaged, too. That man and his team are good. Really good." William spoke with true admiration.

Clarisse's floor was finished as well. Her walls were almost complete. The sewing room floor had been finished. Aunt Belle's and Charlie's room still had to be done. As fast as they were working, they would have all the fireplace floors and walls finished in another day or two. I was anxious to know the final decision on the placement of the upstairs bath and closets.

"Hey Clarisse? Are you here? Did you do the drawing? I can bring you some more pencils and a better pad to use. Do you want me to do that?"

I sat down on her bed and picked up her baby doll. I moved the small cross back into the center of the doll's chest. "Clarisse, do you sleep with your baby in this bed? You have come downstairs and gotten in bed with me, haven't you? I don't mind. Did Morton touch you? Does he bother you now?"

William stopped in the doorway. Suddenly the smell rushed past him into the Clarisse's room. It was so strong I gagged. William grabbed my arm and pulled me up from the bed. "Go downstairs now."

The first floor had clean smelling air. I sat in the closest chair I could reach. I put my head between my knees and tried to breath. I was nauseated, and I had a sick headache.

William brought me some water. "I think you hit the nail on the head. Morton was sexually abusing Clarisse. He didn't want you to find out. He drove you out from upstairs. I don't know if Clarisse would be able to tell you anything, but he was afraid she would."

"Do you want to go back to your place in town? It might be best since Morton is riled up tonight."

Both cats were standing at William's feet. He had his hand on my back. I lifted my head and took a deep breath. "Whew. I think I am okay now. Man, that was one of the worse stinks he's made. Let me lay down for a minute. I'm kind of dizzy. My head is killing me."

I drank the glass of water. Ramona jumped into my lap. William took the dust sheets off Belle's bed and turned the covers back. I took a couple of Tylenol and lay back on the pillows. I was still holding Clarisse's baby doll.

We had planned to stay the night together. I hated to lose this infrequent chance to be with him. Maybe it was best we go back to our houses.

I shut my eyes. I felt William lay down beside me. I rolled over to place my head on his shoulder. There wasn't a shoulder. There wasn't a William when I opened my eyes. William was sitting in a chair next to the bed.

"Didn't you just get in the bed and lay down?"

He looked puzzled. "What? No, I got this chair out of the kitchen and sat down. I thought you might go to sleep, and I didn't want you to be alone."

"Where are the cats?" I asked. "Are they in the bed?"

"Both of them are here with me. Ramona is in my lap. Randolph is laying on my feet. Why, Patty?"

"I am not alone in this bed. I think Clarisse came down with us when Morton showed out. I have her doll. I think she got in the bed with me."

"I think I want to go back to town, William. Do you mind? I just don't feel very comfortable here." I laid Clarisse's doll down on Belle's bed.

"No, Honey. Come on. I agree. I am going to follow you home. After I know you're settled in and okay, I'll go back to my place for the night."

# CHAPTER 80

The next morning William called. "Honey, how are you? Did you get any sleep?"

"I did, but it took forever to fall asleep. The cats are still in the bed. They stayed up with me for a long time. I'll meet you at Belle's place in about an hour if that's okay with you."

The cats and I got out of the car. Tony and Hal were there. They had let the chickens out and fed them. Guinea Girl was chatting away. I guess nothing had happened in her world last night. My world felt definitely off kilter.

"What are y'all up to?" I asked them. I didn't have a great deal of enthusiasm for the day.

"We thought we would work on all the brush around the shed. I have Daddy's small chain saw." Tony lifted the saw.

I cringed. "Have you ever used that before? Does your daddy know you have it?"

"Yes, Ma'am, Daddy's upstairs. He told me that I could use it, but Hal has to be with me all the time. We both have to have our cells phones on. We can't do anything but work on the stuff at the shed. We have to use the loppers and shears first. If we have something too big for the loppers, we can use it then. I have to call Daddy and tell him I am going to crank it. Hal has to stay on the phone until I finish with the chain saw. Daddy is worse than Mama on stuff like this."

'You've got a good daddy. I'd rather you not use that thing. William is coming over in a little bit. Maybe he can go down there with you. I trust you and Hal to look after yourselves, but that saw is dangerous. I am scared you might get hurt."

The boys gave me such a look. I know they were rolling their eyes as they headed off to the back lot.

William rolled in a few minutes later. One of the men was carrying in lumber. William grabbed some more and headed upstairs. I could hear them all talking. I put the coffee on and got out some frozen sweet rolls. By the time they needed a break the sweet rolls would be thawed, and the coffee would be welcome.

I called Keith at the antique store and asked about the stain glass. He still had it and another piece. They were a pair. I hadn't realized there were two of them. The bathroom downstairs wouldn't be able to use but one. Maybe I could use the other piece upstairs. I asked Keith if he would measure them and call me back. I'd talk to either Horace or the framer about them.

"Patty, there isn't any smell upstairs. Maybe Morton burned himself out last night."

I laughed "From your lips to God's ears"

"I think it is Satan not God that Morton has a deal with." William laughed. "Is the coffee ready. I slipped out this morning without eating anything."

I poured him coffee and put the plate of sweet rolls on the table. I wished I had some of Ring-a-ding's biscuits.

My biscuits were awful. I stood by Ring-a-ding's side and watched her make them. She stood by my side while I made them. Little white rocks. I can't tell you how many times I tried. "Baby, I just don't understand it. I watched you every step of the way. You just didn't inherit the biscuit making gene. These are edible, they just are not……perfect."

That was her nice way of telling me they were either hard as a rock or gummy in the middle. Either way, not fit to eat. The chickens liked them though.

"William, ask if anyone wants coffee and sweet rolls upstairs. Then will you go down to the shed and check on the boys. Tell them to come eat something if they want. And, William, Tony has a chain saw. He has really strict instructions on when he can use it from Darryl. I'm a little scared of them cranking it though. Would you check on them about that, too?"

Randolph and Ramona wandered in the back door as William departed. Randolph stuck his foot in the empty crunchy dish. I refilled it and gave them fresh water. Both cats settled down in front of the old stove to nibble.

"BOOM!"

I jumped three feet in the air and went running out of the kitchen door. Darryl was coming down the steps and passed me, jumping off the porch. I heard other footfalls clamoring behind us.

I was close behind Darryl when we got to the new barn. "Patty, stay back here." He ordered.

"That was a gun shot. I'm right behind you." I didn't even break stride.

I saw William and the boys in the field. No one looked like he was bleeding.

"What the hell was that? Are you okay? Who fired that shot gun?" Darryl was in good shape to be able to say all that while running at top speed.

"I did, Darryl. Everyone is okay. It was a rattler. Slow down." William was walking toward us, carrying the breached shot gun over his arm.

When we reached him, he handed Darryl the gun. "We were lucky Tony had pulled the truck down here today. He had the shot gun in the window rack." The boys were wearing snake boots. William was wearing high topped leather work boots. The snake could have struck above his boot line but hopefully wouldn't have reached that high. We both needed to buy snake boots if we were going to go out in the back lot.

We walked over to the snake—dead, but still writhing. Those muscles don't get the message the head is gone. The head is still dangerous, too.

The venom in a rattle snake is very toxic. The muscles in the head and jaws can still pump poison long after it is dead.

The body was over five feet long. It had been separated about six or eight inches from the head.

The others from the house had reached us. They all began telling snake stories and complimented William on his fine shooting.

"Mr. William, can I have it? I am learning taxidermy. I will mount it for you. You can put in the house. That is a trophy snake. I can sew the head back on and glue it all to a Styrofoam form. You'll never know it was in two parts. I can make it look like it is about to strike." Walter was practically twitching with excitement.

I thought to myself, "Oh, no. Only over my dead body will that thing come into the house."

William looked at my face. "Walter, why don't you take the snake home with you? You can have it to practice your taxidermy skills. Put it in your workshop."

I sighed a deep sigh.

Everyone finally got tired of looking at the snake and wandered back to the house. Walter would come back with a box for the snake when it stopped moving around. I knew we had snakes, but I hadn't seen one in a long time. I hadn't thought about one being that large. I guess the bush hogging had stirred this one up. If one was around, there would be more. That shed was probably inhabited by a large family of them. The boys and I were going to have a talk about their project.

Everyone sat down on the porch and drank coffee or cokes. I started another pot of coffee. While it perked, I joined the men on the porch. The snake stories had morphed into other stories. They were laughing and telling taller and taller tales.

# CHAPTER 81

Mr. Horace came out the kitchen door. "What's going on? Are we having a coffee break?" Mr. Horace had his own cup of coffee in his hand. He was smiling at everyone.

The men thanked me for the drinks and good naturedly went back to work. Tony and Hal started telling Mr. Horace about the snake. Walter, Toby, Mr. Horace, William, and the boys headed to back to view the carcass. I thought Mr. Horace might be disappointed to find only a five-or-six- foot rattlesnake. The boys made it sound as if it was twenty feet long with eight-inch fangs.

I stepped out on to the back porch steps and rang the old farm bell. Everyone would be back at the house in a few minutes.

I dished up the food for William, the boys, and Mr. Horace. I took my plate to my regular place at the table. I asked Mr. Horace about William's idea of using the stain glass. Keith called about that time with the measurements.

Horace did some figuring and said. "That'll work out just fine. Depending on where we place the shower stall, you could put the stain glass over on the toilet upstairs. Are you still going to put only a shower upstairs? If you do that, we could place that second glass vertically instead of horizontally. Think about that. Chalk it off where you want it, and we'll do some figuring."

The boys went back to the shed with strong warnings about the snakes. The three of us went upstairs to Morton's room. A faint aroma was wafting through the air.

Mr. Horace said the original plans for the bathroom placement were still the best. He took out some blue tape and marked the outer wall. "This is how far into this room the bathroom wall will come. You have the rest of the space for a small room and a closet or just one big closet. If it was me, I'd put in a big closet. You could run a rod down both sides of the room. I'd put shelves under the window and on door side of the room."

A huge closet. Oh, I was liking this plan.

"Patty, when Miss Belle rewired the house and updated the kitchen and bathroom, I ran electricity to the old barn." Darryl had joined us. "There is a pole with a light on it about halfway between the new barn and the crib. I think the power company would turn that back on. The light needs to be replaced, I'm sure. It would probably cost you $5 or $10.00 a month. I pay $8.00 extra for the light I have in back of the house where my workshop is.'

"If they'll turn that light one, I can run power to anything you want outside. Tony said you want lights in the new barn. I can put you some florescent fixtures in the stall side and in the first and second floors. We can place a master switch up here in the house so you can turn everything on and off without having to go to the barn. I can put motion lights on the corners of the new barn and one at the peak of the crib. With the pole light you only need to put one set of motion lights on the far-right side of the new barn. How about one of the motion lights on the hen house? That'd scare a fox off. Any other place you want outside lights, you just let me know."

## CHAPTER 82

I went downstairs to call the Electric Membership Corporation. After a few minutes they had the account up. The lady on the phone scheduled a technician to come out and look things over. If they can do it, it would only cost an extra $8.00 a month, which would be added to my regular electric bill. We set up a time for the EMC men to install the pole light.

I cleaned up the kitchen and made a grocery list. I really didn't need anything much at my house in town. If I was going to have people in and out of this place, I needed some groceries. I was down to only enough grounds for one more pot of coffee. That was dire.

I grabbed my purse and told William where I was going. I ran by my house and checked the larder. Adding few things to the list, I stopped at the Piggly Wiggly. I bought the two biggest packages of 8 O'clock coffee I could find. It may have been summer, but the coffee pot seemed to always be in demand. I bought several more cases of drinks and water. The bakery lady was putting fresh chocolate chip cookies out. I couldn't resist those.

I put lunch meat, bread, and condiments on the table on the back porch. I had bar-b-que and plain potato chips. The chocolate chip cookies from the bakery were still warm and fragrant. Sweet tea was made. Cokes were in the refrigerator. Let the locust come.

I rang the bell. In a minute Hal and Tony came up. They did a preliminary cleaning at the faucet outside. I sent them to the sink with hot water and a "Wash those hands good and clean. Get your fingernails, too, and wash your faces."

I gave William the same instructions when he got there. "Yes, Ma'am," they all said.

After everyone had eaten, William wrapped things for the refrigerator while I put up the other items. We went to the back porch and sat in the rockers. I had a sweet tea, and he had a Coke. We each had a lap full of cat.

"What have you been doing?" I asked.

"Nothing much. Mostly I've been trying to stay out of the way. I helped Walter and Toby put in the outhouse floor and remount the door. Did you know the crescent moon is cut backwards?"

"Yep, Uncle Charlie did that a hundred years ago. He had the door face down, not face up. He didn't know it was backwards until it was hung. Ring-a-ding liked it. She said it was a sign Charlie wasn't as perfect as he thought he was. She always knew he was a bit 'bass ackwards.'"

Did you find your tote bag?" asked William.

"I'm glad you said that. I would like to slide the beds out far enough to get into the chifforobe. I am pretty sure it is on the floor on the hanging side of the wardrobe. I can see it in my mind. It has Belle's stuff from the vault. I need to take it out of the house. I probably should put it back into the bank deposit box. Tomorrow I'll try to drop it all by the bank."

While William went to the back lot, I went to Belle's bedroom. I needed to replace the dust sheets so any dirt from upstairs would not settle on it. The bed covers were still pulled back, and you could see where my head had been. The other pillow had an indention in it. Was that from Clarisse, or had it already been there? I pulled the covers back into place. I spread the dust sheets over the bed.

"Wait a minute. Where was Clarisse's baby doll? I know it was on the bed when we left last night."

Wasn't it? My head had hurt so badly I didn't' really trust my memory. I was pretty confident I didn't go back upstairs to replace the doll in her bedroom. William was with me the whole time, so he didn't take it up. I had forgotten about it this morning. I looked under the bed. The cats had not knocked it onto the floor.

I was getting pretty good at this girding my loins business. I was ready for the next surprise. So up the steps I headed.

# CHAPTER 83

The doll wasn't on the bed. There was a lump under the dust sheet. There she sat. She was sitting propped up against the pillow with Clarisse's little Bible. The dust sheet had been pulled over her and the pillows. Clarisse had put her baby to bed.

"Hey Clarisse, I am glad you took your baby back to your bed. I am sorry I carried her off in my panic last night. I brought you some crayons and a drawing pad. Can you read and write? You can draw me pictures if you want to." I was speaking really softly. I didn't want the men working upstairs to think I was fruit-loopy even though I was beginning to think I was. I laid the pad and crayons on the foot of her bed and left the room.

They were putting up the frame for the bathroom wall. It looked huge, but once all the fixtures were in it wouldn't be that big. It was going to be a nice addition to the house.

I had decided to go with the full room being a closet. I think that would maximize the space. Shelving under the window would give some space for folded things. I thought I might place one of the chifforobes against the wall next to the door. Once we had everything moved in, I might consider putting drawers or shelving down the center space. I'd have to live with it first though.

I had taken one of the crayons for Clarisse's box. I asked the men doing the framing to show me where the toilet, sink, and shower would be. I wasn't good at visualizing how much space each item would take.

One of the men took out a chunk of blue chalk. "You don't want to use a crayon on these floors.' He said. Using the chalk, he drew a box with a "T" in it. "This is the toilet and you need to allow this much space on the front and sides. Here is the shower. You want this much space in front of it. You need less space if you use sliding doors instead of the kind that open up." Marking a "VS" for vanity and sink, he marked off another space. "Does this tell you what you want?"

"Yes, Sir, it does. Will the window stay there over the toilet?" I asked.

"Unless you want us to remove it, Horace allowed for it to stay. It gives you good light in here. Personally, I'd leave it and the ones in the bedroom/closet space."

I agreed with him about the windows. I didn't think the stain glass panel needed to be in this bathroom. I would put one of them on the outside wall of the downstairs bath. I didn't want to break up the pair of art glass windows if I could use the second one. I went downstairs searching for possible locations. I looked at the big window in the kitchen. If the glass panel could be hung so it would be the top part of the window, I thought it would be pretty. It wouldn't go from edge to edge. It would make sort of a center piece like a valance. It could be a beautiful addition to the room. It would not block the view into the side garden. That was settled. That's where the second stained glass would go.

I called Keith. I asked him to set both stain glass windows aside for me. I'd drop by and pay him for them later.

I was feeling really positive about the house today. Thinking about the colors in the stain glass, I decided to paint the Pepto-Bismol pink kitchen a soft apricot or a peach color. With a pale, not an intense color, and with white fixtures, counters, and baseboards, the room would be much brighter. I could tell a huge difference with the glass shelves off the windows. I might put one shelf back in the window. If it were placed either in the middle or toward the bottom of the windows, I could keep some of Ring-a-dings flowers there. Her philodendron could trail from the antique stove as she always had it. I would move the old stove against the outside kitchen wall to give a bit more room. It had been left sitting catty-cornered in the room to cover the old hot water heater. That would not be needed anymore as we installed an immediate demand water system.

While I was dreaming of this new bright kitchen, I cleaned the old stove of all its stuff. The stove tended to catch things as you came in the back door. I had a stack of mail, a bowl with keys, and dead leaves from the plants that had been moved outside. Aunt Belle had kept some of her cast iron pans in the oven. I looked through everything. I put a few back, but most of the things had seen better days. I kept the old iron frying pans and the kettle. The kettle would stay on the top of the stove. I might display a couple of the iron pans on the wall. Maybe. I wasn't so sure I liked that idea.

I know! I have Mama's collection of 1940's and 50's china tomatoes. She had a sugar bowl, a creamer, and a tray plus some small hors d'oeuvres knives and forks with vegetable handles. There were two sets of salt and pepper shakers shaped like bell peppers. I think one of those sets had a tray as well. They would go here on the stove. I also had Mama and Daddy's collection of porcelain birds. Those would go throughout the house. I would use those extra shelves in the sunroom for their birds and some of Belle's violets. I was excited to bring some of my parents' things into my living space again.

William came in. He and the kids had been down at the shed. "The boys are coming in a minute. They were pulling the rest of the brush away. I used the chain saw. Not the boys."

"No more snakes today?" I asked. He drank two glasses of water before he answered.

"No. None, today. Thank goodness. The back end of the shed is clear. The inside has to be cleaned out before we can really get to the car to pull it out."

"Hey, Miss Patricia. Did Mr. William tell you we can get all the way inside the shed?" Hall burst through the kitchen door. Tony was right behind him.

The boys' conversations spilled over each other as they told me the shed had old tires, part of a bicycle, and a bunch of mason jars. No surprise there! There was no telling what was in that shed.

"Clean up. If you want something to eat, there are peanut butter and vanilla wafers on the back porch. Help yourself. Get some water. It is hot today. There is a grocery list pad on the refrigerator. Please remember to write down things when you see we need something."

We ate a few cookies and sat on the back porch. At least I was able to make sure this way they were drinking plenty of water. The boys chattered on about the car. When they finished, they rushed back off to the shed.

"You watch for snakes and spiders. Wear gloves; be careful. Keep your phones on." I yelled to their disappearing backsides.

"I'm going back down there. I think it is too dangerous for them to be by themselves. Do you need me up here for anything?" William said as he put his dishes in the dishwasher. "I'm taking that case of bottled water with me. We forgot it this morning."

"Wait a second, William. I want to tell you about Clarisse and her baby doll."

"This is good. We know Clarisse is friendly and likes you, Honey. Maybe she can help fight Morton for us."

"No, I don't think she can. She is scared of him. She is looking to me for protection. We have to get rid of Morton so she will feel safe. As far as I am concerned, Clarisse can stay with us. Morton needs to go. Before you go back down to the boys, help me move these beds so I can get to the chifforobe."

Those old wrought iron beds were heavy. I should have gotten the boys to help us. I tried to pick up one end, and it was almost more than I could do. William stopped me and got the moving pads. He lifted the corners, and I slipped the pads under the feet. We slid both beds out. They would have to be put back this afternoon in case someone needed to get into the bathroom.

William pulled the coverings off the chifforobe. I was able to reach in and grab my tote bag. I also got the folders I had left with it. We recovered the wardrobe and slid the beds back against it. The bathroom was now open for business.

# CHAPTER 84

I carried the stuff into the kitchen. I had managed to keep the kitchen fairly clean of the debris from upstairs by keeping the door closed. I was running the vacuum cleaner in there a couple of times a day.

Mr. Fordham, a master brick mason, was closing the kitchen fireplace in today. He had spent the last two days repointing the brick work in the front room fireplace. He had left the brick work around it, but it was not a working fireplace. It would accept a decorative false front, now.

We had decided to use one of the Victorian metal coal fireplace fronts in the chimney opening. The original mantel would be returned. The fire screen looked great. All the pieces had been under the house. Mr. Fordham, who was supervising the chimney work, picked the screen up. "Patricia, you know what this is?" I had to admit I didn't.

Mr. Fordham explained they were used by Victorians to help hold heat. They were cast iron. He said most of them were used with coal fires but not always. He said they were decorative and useful. With his advice, we decided to use one in the front fireplace. It would look as if a Victorian fireplace had been installed in our wood burning fireplace. He had some additional pieces in his shed to "Fix it right up and make it purr-ty."

I walked out on the front porch and looked at the mantel. It had been painted dark brown years ago. I had thought about painting it white. Maybe it could be cleaned and returned to its natural colored wood.

I called Mr. Casper and asked him if he would look at the front room mantel. I told him it was painted, but I wondered if he thought it could be cleaned.

"You bring it over here, Patty. If'n I can't strip back to natural, I'll paint it for you. I gots me a professional paint sprayer that will make it look shiny just like glass." He was so excited.

William and the boys took it over to his house. Miss Rachel sent them back with peach pies. "Miss Rachel is going to have me fat as a hog. She just sings and cooks sweets all day. I found her reading yesterday. She was

smiling and reading a murder who-dun-it. I asked if it was a good book."
William was smiling as he told me.

"Yeah, it's okay. The house is so quiet now I can read. Y'all keep finding Casper things to do."

"I told her I would try. I have never seen her so happy, Honey."

There wasn't a pretty mantel in the kitchen. It was one board coming across and two coming down the side to cover the margins where the brick and wall met. The mantel was a single pine shelf. All the wood had been painted ugly dark brown. That was the same thing in all the rooms upstairs, too. They were just functional and not decorative in any way. The front room was the only mantel with any style at all.

Mr. Fordham called me over. "Patty, there is granite under this hearth. It probably is cracked, and that is why concrete was poured over it. You care if I chisel this old cement out? I think the granite hearth would be prettier than filling this in with wood. Would you consider leaving the kitchen fireplace open instead of putting another Victorian face in here? You could put in gas logs. You can't burn real wood anymore, but I can vent gas logs outside. You can prop that old screen beside it for decoration."

I felt as if Mr. Fordham knew a lot more about these things than I did. I agreed to all he wanted to do. I thought it would be beautiful.

"Mr. Fordham? Could I put another kind of mantel up there? I was going to paint all the trim white with a pale peachy/apricot wall color. Would it best to leave this original mantel?"

"That kind of mantel is typical of what you had in these old houses. Only the best room would have had a fancy mantel. I pulled the boards off to get to the sides. If you want, you can put up a full mantel like the one in the front room. It's just whatever you want, Patty. You can do anything. This is your place now."

Well, yes, it was. It wasn't Belle's place anymore. It was William's and mine now.

"I don't want to hurt your feelings none, Patty, but I got to tell you, this pink room is ugly. I know Belle loved it, but anything you do in here would be an improvement."

I had to laugh. "When she picked out the color, I tried to tell her it was going to be really dark and bold. I asked her to choose a lighter version, but nope. This was it. I don't think she was as happy with it after it was painted. She was just too stubborn to admit she had made a mistake."

I pulled the shop vacuum cleaner over to him. He began chiseling and sucking up pieces of concrete. "Here's the crack. It is in the back and won't never show. I'll get the rest of this concrete out of here and check the back bricks. I think you will be really glad you left this granite exposed. I have some stuff that will clean these old bricks and granite. They won't' look like new, but they will look better. There won't be none of that sooty residue."

Mr. Fordham continued chipping away. "I think you'd be happier with a fancy mantel piece. You like pretty stuff, and this ain't all that pretty. Go find one and let me know what the measures are for the opening. That way I can fix it in so's the bricks will line up like they are supposed to."

I walked down to the shed where a growing pile of trash and junk was forming. William and the boys were sitting on the truck tail gate drinking water.

"Hey, y'all, isn't it too hot for you out here? Don't you need to quit and rest for a while?" I asked.

"We have got to go help my daddy this afternoon. He is cleaning up and organizing the shed by his workshop. He bought a new truck for the big electrical work. He wants us to help fix a parking space for it. He said he'd be back early this afternoon. I guess we ought to pack up. I wish we could get that car out." Said Tony.

"The car has been here forever, and it will be here forever more. It isn't going anywhere. Let's quit. When y'all get things done for Darryl, we can start again, Tony." William said as he started picking up water bottles.

"Is there anyone who takes old tires? I hate to leave all this mess out here in the field." I asked.

Hal said "We are going to clean it up, Miss Patricia. Don't worry. There is a lot of glass co-cola bottles, metal cans, and just trash. We can take it all to the recycling place in town. Over in Chester is a place that grinds up tires to make mulch. They'll pay us 20 cents for each tire."

The boys left. William and I went back to the house. "I want to ride into town to the antique shop. Want to go? Mr. Fordham and I have been talking about putting a different mantel in the kitchen. Keith might have one or know where I could find a pretty piece."

"Let me take a shower and get cleaned up. I smell worse than Morton on one of his bad days." William lifted his arm and fanned his hand toward me.

"OH, MY GAWD! I may not be able to marry you after that! You stink to high heaven. I am surprised the buzzards aren't circling overhead thinking you are a dead possum or something."

# CHAPTER 85

After showering and putting on some clean jeans and t-shirt, we told Mr. Fordham we were leaving. "Here, you take these measures. Don't get nothing any bigger'n this. It can be twelve feet tall, but the sides have to fit right 'chere, like this." He drew an imaginary mantel out with his hands.

I gathered up the folders and my tote bag. William put his nasty clothes in a plastic bag and locked them in the trunk. "I don't want even a whiff of your el stinko in this car." I sneered. He made a snarky face.

"Go by my house. I'll check on the kitties and throw your clothes in the washing machine. I need to do a load of my work clothes, too. I want to change. I am awfully dusty from being in the floor with Mr. Fordham. Did you know Toby who is working with Walter is Mr. Fordham's grandson? I swear you can't spit without hitting a relative."

The cats were curled up on my bed. They came running into the kitchen when we came in. Sniffs, purrs, and rubbing ensued with lots of "Did you miss us?" baby talk from the humans. They followed William into the laundry room. As soon as he opened that bag of dirty clothes, they took one sniff and ran back to the kitchen.

"I must have awfully powerful sweat glands. Not even Ramona would have anything to do with me."

I took a quick shower and put on fresh clothes. "William, I left my tote bag and stuff in the car. Would you bring it in for me? I won't be another minute." I poured some fresh treats and water for the cats. I emptied the dryer from last night's washing.

At Keith's store I looked at the two pieces of stain glass again. I was sure I wanted them for the kitchen and the downstairs bath. Keith pulled them out and marked them sold for me. "Leave them here until you are ready to install them. If you want to hang one of them in the kitchen, look here. At one time, they both hung in a window. I think they were meant to be vertical, but they were hung horizontally. The pattern isn't bothered by the direction. This is the one you want to hang. It still has a good frame and the chains for hanging are still there. The other one has had the hooks for the chains to pull out. I would put that permanently in as a window."

I asked him about mantels. "I have two in the back. They are nice but not really fancy. Come on back here and look at these." I explained where the mantel would go.

"Beatrice is working this afternoon. She ought to be here in about thirty minutes. If you want to kill some time, we can drive over to my storage shed. I have two or three mantels there. There is one that I am thinking about. It would need refinishing. It has the egg and dart carving around the mirror and bell flowers going down the front legs. It is a pretty mantel. It's been painted several times. I scrapped around one of the bell flowers. Someone put gold paint on them. That is the hardest stuff to get off. It can be done, but it is a terror."

We left Keith to his other customers and roamed around the shop. He had some intriguing items. If I decided I was going to get rid of any of the antiques I had, I would call Keith. We looked in the vintage jewelry display cabinets. I love vintage jewelry. He had a number of broaches like Ring-a-ding's. Some had impressive price tags.

"See anything you can't live without?" asked Keith.

"Do people really pay these prices for this jewelry and old broaches?" I was amazed.

"Yeah, they sure do and more. I sell a lot of them at the Scott Antique Market in Atlanta, and I have an online store, too. There are people who just collect cameos, or broaches, or just vintage things in one color. You'd be amazed. Go with me next time. You'd have a ball and spend all of William's money, too."

"Looking in this case, I realize that I have a fortune upstairs in Belle's toolbox. I wish I could do something to display them." I mused.

"You got an old picture frame? Let me show you something." Keith took us into the work room in the back. "I haven't finished this one, but look at that."

Someone had attached old broaches, earrings, pendants and pieces of gold chain to a framed piece of pale green canvas. The jewelry made a floral pattern. Some chains had been added to look like long leaves. They were fascinating.

"Do you think I could use some of Belle's things and do something similar?"

Keith picked up the piece that wasn't finished. "Sure, you can. Look at the back of this. See how the pins are mounted. Use strong thread. I have found some evidence of glue. Now there were some pieces on the first one that were broken. Those were glued in with jewelry paste. So far, I haven't found any paste on this one. The paste hadn't gotten brittle, discolored, or cracked. These were done in 1967. The woman who made them signed and dated them. I can order you the right kind of glue. Don't use just anything. I am thinking about taking this old oval gold frame and making one of just odd and broken pieces I have. You come help me with it. We'll learn together."

Keith was one of my favorite people. He made me laugh when no one else could. He and Belle would regularly visit on the phone. You could always tell when it was her "boyfriend." You could hear her laughing a mile away.

He had been after her to sell him Uncle Charlie's roll top desk for years. I knew he would start on me soon. It was an impressive thing. It was a massive desk. The entire front opened to reveal the desk inside, with drawers and pigeon-holes. I had never seen another quite like it. I think it was Uncle Charlie's father's or his grandfather's, maybe. I needed to research it. Add one more thing to my to-do list.

Belle had made a notebook with all the information I needed for her funeral. There was another book titled "furniture and stuff." Years ago, when she first created it, she had shown me the notebook. She had listed all the important things in the house and written a description about them. She said it would be good for future generations. I was sure she had information on Uncle Charlie's desk.

# CHAPTER 86

Keith didn't have a storage building. He had a huge barn, and it was filled to the brim. "Watch that vat. It has some chemical stripper in it. Come on back. Watch where you walk. Here they are." Keith was dancing between pieces of furniture and boxes.

Three mantels were propped against the wall. We moved some things away from them so we could see them better. 'This one, Puddin'. I think this is the one you need." Keith pointed to the mantel with the mirror. "I wouldn't even change the mirror. It is the original beveled glass. There are not any cracks. The silvering is a bit damaged in this lower left side, but it is over a hundred years old. I just might be a little damaged when I get that old."

It was a lovely mantel. William pulled out Mr. Fordham's measurements. He and Keith compared the openings and sizes to Mr. Fordham's list. It complied with the requirements.

Keith pointed out the gilding and explained about the cleaning. He showed us the back and how sturdy it was. "This is the best mantel I have. It is in good condition. I know you like flowers and fancy stuff, Puddin'. I would strip it. Use a good stain and varnish; this will be a show piece. The reason I haven't put it in the shop is because I was going to clean and fix it up first. If you want it, I'll make you a great deal on it."

Keith and William loaded the mantel into Keith's truck. We headed toward Belle's place. "William, is Puddin' always this bossy? You might better rethink that proposal? You get her riled up, and you had best head for the hills. I know this girl." Keith was pointing at me. Keith and I had known each other all our lives. He and Pickle were the only people who still called me Puddin'.

Mr. Fordham's truck was parked in the front yard. I ran up the front porch steps. "Mr. Fordham, we found a mantel. What do you think?"

He came out carrying his tape measure. It met with his approval. "Do you want to clean it first, or you want me to go on and put it in?"

"Mr. Casper has the organ and the front room mantel. I thought I'd ask him if he would consider cleaning and refinishing this one, too. I thought we'd take it over to him while it is on Keith's truck if you think it will work."

"Yep, take it on over to Casper. He does good work. I know he hates retirement. Child, you may just have given him a new career." Mr. Fordham slapped Keith on the back and went back in the house.

Miss Rachel was watering her flowers on the porch when we drove up. "What y'all got? Come in this house. I made an old-fashioned chocolate cake this morning. I have been wanting some of that boiled chocolate icing. You don't know how happy you have made Ghostly and me." She sang out.

"Ghostly? Is that Mr. Casper?" I asked.

"With a name like Casper, how could it be anyone else? I've been calling him Ghostly since our courting days. You just ain't heard it because I do it mostly when we are alone. He kind of likes it, but he won't admit it." Turning to the intercom, she pressed a button "Ghostly! Come in the house."

"He'll be here in a minute. Tell me you got something else for him to do. He has had a ball with that old organ. I saw it last night. It is a pretty thing. It's still in two pieces. He is rebuilding the bellows now. I think that's all that's left to do before putting it back together."

"What you want, Woman?" Mr. Casper came smiling into the kitchen. "Well, I am glad to see you. I was going to call you. I want you to come see the organ. I am about to set the bellows in to see if'n they fit. If'n they do, we are ready to put her together and take her home."

After some of the best chocolate cake I have ever eaten, we went to the workshop. The organ was beautiful. The mirror had a little hazing, but the finish of the wood was soft and lovely. "Mr. Casper. YOU are a true artist." I sighed.

"Yep, I enjoyed this, Patty. It looks good if'n I do say so myself. William, you get over here. Keith, you hold the base still. Let's slide the bellows in and see if'n it fits."

It did. I asked Mr. Casper if he could keep the organ a few more days. I hated to bring it back into all that dust.

"Sure, it is fine where it is. We'll move it against that wall out of the way 'til you want it to come home."

"I got another goodie for you if you want it." I teased.

"What you got, Child? You just working me to death." Mr. Casper gripped as we went to Keith's truck. "You women, just keep finding stuff for me to do."

"MMMMMM. Nice mantel piece. This here come from you, Keith?"

"Yes, Sir." Keith said absent mindedly from the garage door.

Casper looked it over. "Walnut. I like me a good piece of walnut furniture. You wants me to fix this one up, too?"

"If you would like to do it, I wish you would." I looked over toward Rachel who was nodding her head yes.

The men took the new mantel in and laid it on a pair of sawhorses. Running his hands over it, Mr. Casper looked very pleased. "You gonna leave this nature-colored? If'n I was you, I would. A little walnut stain and a good varnish, mm-hmmm. Yeah, this here will be something else to see. I see some dang fool done put gold paint on it. I can get rid of that in no time. It's a pain, but it can be done. UMM-hmmm, yes sir. This is going to be even purdier than that there other one."

I wasn't sure, but I think Mr. Casper was purring.

"I'm gonna do this 'un next. That mantel piece over yonder can wait. It don't need as much tending to as this one. Kitchen, huh? Yeah, that'll look good in there. Ummm-hmm, mighty fine." He was already reaching for a tiny tool to pick at the finish.

"I can't thank you enough, Mr. Casper. Miss Rachel, the house is a mess, but when it is all done, I want you to come see it."

"Patty, we'll come. Thank you for getting Ghostly outta his funk. He was so down and miserable. I couldn't do nothing for him. I was getting really worried. You have brought him back to life."

William and I hugged Rachel. We began walking toward truck. Keith was nowhere to be seen. "He's in the workshop with Mr. Casper." William pointed.

"Oh, they are talking. Think we should interrupt?" William took my hand and led me into the shop. Rachel noticed and started walking in that direction, too.

"You do beautiful work, Mr. Casper. If you will take on the repairs and refinishing of my stuff, I will pay you well. Right now, I have twin headboards that would be stunning as a king size bed. It would take a master carpenter to blend them together. Could you do that? And there is a lovely old chest of drawers, but the supports have come loose, and one the drawers is broken. Can you come by the store and look at it? And would you come out to my storage place? I have more in there. I just can't get it all done."

"Oh, Mr. Casper, I have people who come by the shop and ask me about pieces they have that need special repairs or refinishing. I can refer people to you. Would you want me to do that?" Keith was talking just as fast as a southern drawl would allow.

"Well now, Young'un, I suppose I could. Patty's stuff comes first. I ain't got nothin' going on after that. If'n I could come in and see them beds, I bet I could make it work. I can come in tomorrow, and we can talk. Once I get Patty's stuff done and out, you can bring me the things a couple of pieces at a time. You got someone who can help you with lifting, don't cha? I can't do a lot of heavy lifting no more. That's why I had to retire. If'n my back would have held out, I'd have stayed on the job. I work on Patty's things for a time, and then I sits down if'n I need to. I work on my own time now."

"You come tomorrow to look through the store. Then we can go over to my storage shed. You tell me the things you want to work on and when you want them. I have been trying to redo and repair things, but I am not master craftsman like you. I need your expertise. You will save me time, and time is money. You and Rachel come in the morning and I will take you to lunch and we'll talk about everything." Keith said, shaking Mr. Casper's hand.

Rachel was standing at the door. She had her hands under her apron as if she was praying. "Keith, come in the house a minute. She wrapped up the remainder of the chocolate cake and gave it to him. She was crying and hugging him at the same time. You and Patty have saved me from the 'lectric chair. If you hadn't come along, I'd have killed him by now."

Keith was so overcome he could only stammer, "Yes'm" over and over again.

We were laughing all the way back to the shop. "Man, was Rachel happy or what?" Keith said.

"Hey, it was my idea first. Hand over that cake." I laughed.

"Rachel will keep you in sweets for the rest of your life. My bedroom smells like a bakery all the time now." William laughed.

"Beatrice, put the coffee on. Come eat cake. It's chocolate!" Keith sang coming in the door.

"Cake? I'll make coffee right this minute." Beatrice shuffled off to the back room. Beatrice had broken her ankle some years ago. She wears this heavy boot like thing. To make it prettier, she pins broaches to the fabric or ties ribbons on it. If she can find earrings and a matching pin, she is in hog heaven. She is one of the most entertaining people I know. Beatrice and Belle always had jokes to share.

"Coffee's on. Here are some plates and my finest napkins." She said as she pulled paper towels off a roll. I cut slices of cake, placing them on antique china plates. We sat down at the lovely dining room table in the show room.

Keith told Beatrice about the deal he had worked out with Casper. We got the giggles as he told her about Rachel, the cake, and the electric chair.

"Good. You need to be more available for buying and selling. Casper was miserable when the doctor told him he had to retire. Casper will enjoy having something productive to do, and he can make some extra money. Did you know that Rachel is baking birthday cakes for people these days? I wonder if I could get her to do me one of these chocolate cakes every week." Beatrice was not missing a single crumb. "This is the kind of old-fashioned icing my mama used to cook. I haven't had it in years." Beatrice said with a dreamy look on her face.

# CHAPTER 87

"Where to now, Kemosabe?"

"Let's go back to my house unless you have something else to do." I suggested.

"I'm pooped." William said as he took off his loafers and put his feet on the ottoman. Please tell me you are taking this chair to Belle's."

"If you want it, it comes to Belle's place with us." I heard him sigh. I looked at him, and he was asleep. Ramona had jumped in his lap. Randolph had stretched out full length above his head on the back of the chair. William had not moved one muscle as Ramona settled in.

I laid the folders from Belle's safety deposit box on the table. She had recorded the contents of the house in a notebook. I needed to be sure to save that so that I would have the history. I lay it aside and looked at the other folders. They were mostly papers for which I had duplicates, or they were land deeds. I copied each deed at my computer printer. Punching holes in the duplicates, I put them all in a 3-ring binder. The originals would go back in the vault.

She had some life insurance policies she had listed in her funeral notebook. I made copies of the Death Certificate. I wrote a letter asking for the death benefits from each policy. I was the beneficiary of each one. By the time I had finished those and had them in addressed envelopes, William was snoring to beat the band.

I was glad to get those insurance policies handled. One more job marked off my list. I pulled out a folder that had insurance on the house and all the outbuildings. Looking it over, I decided I needed to increase the coverage. This had been updated when she did all the work with the timber money eight years ago. The house would be worth more with the changes and additions being done to it. I made a note on my to-do list pad to call the insurance carrier.

William drove a mid-size SUV. I had four door sedan. When we married, we needed to put his car and mine on the same policy with the house. I added a comment on my list to check on that when I called the insurance company.

# CHAPTER 88

I started laying out the contents of my tote bag. First was Uncle Charlie's watch. I wound it and held it to my ear. Ticking away just like the day it was put aside. There were old diamond and gold chandelier earrings in a little white cardboard box. They looked like mine-cut or maybe rose cut diamonds. In a little cloth bag was a pair of pearl and diamond earrings. There was a matching pendant rolled in tissue paper. In another bag was a pearl and diamond ring. They made up a set. The ring was too large for Belle but fit my hand perfectly. The earrings were for pierced ears. Belle wore screw back or clip earrings if she wore any at all. Maybe there was a note in her book about to whom these belonged. I bet they were her mother's.

"Take jewelry for cleaning and appraisal" I added to my to-do list.

I put all the jewelry back in their bags and boxes. I placed all that in a quart-sized Ziploc bag. I didn't want the cats to think they had found something fun to bat around.

I stacked the envelopes in a pile. There was a small penknife like the one Belle' kept safety pinned to her apron. It was a pearl handled but was yellowed with age. I opened the blade, and amazingly it was still sharp. I put it in the bag with the jewelry.

I found a tiny cross with a diamond in it. It was very much like the one on Clarisse's baby doll. There was a larger cross without any ornamentation on it, too. I found a small enameled disk that had probably been part of a charm bracelet. It had a link in the hole. There was an old winding key for a watch.

I had made a charm bracelet out of Mama and Daddy's rings when they died. I'd add some of these little items to it. I loved old stuff like this.

William and the cats were still asleep. I just left them alone. I started on the envelopes. A couple were in Uncle Charlie's handwriting. They were statements for land he had paid off or sold. He had several bills of sale for cattle. I didn't think any of that needed to be kept anymore. I put those on the far side of the table. I would check with Alfred before throwing any papers away.

Uncle Charlie had written Belle some love letters. He and Belle wrote in that beautiful old script. Although I knew there was a tender side to Uncle Charlie, I now had proof in his own handwriting. His letters were loving and carefully written. In one, he asked her to marry him when he got home. I am not sure where he was, maybe military service. The ink looked as if it might have been smudged with a few tear drops.

She had some letters from her mother and sisters. There was one from Charlie's mother and several from my grandmother. Inside one of the letters was a pressed flower. My grandmother had written about the beautiful color of the iris. She was saving Belle a rhizome of it, so she could plant one in her yard. There was a lot about flowers and some news about people I didn't know.

After I read each one, I stacked them in a pile, sorting them as to the person who had written the letter. There were three of four more envelopes to go.

In one was a picture drawn by a child. "Clarisse saw Margaret's peacocks today. She drew this picture of one."

It was the picture drawn on the pad. It was Clarisse, not Morton, sending the message. Not a turkey, a peacock. The dots were the eyes of the peacock feathers. Well, of course. Now that I knew what it was, it was unmistakably a peacock.

When I had asked for a clue, she had drawn the peacock. Was Clarisse giving me a clue, or was this the only picture she liked to draw? I think she was telling me to look in my peacock patterned tote bag. All along I had these treasures in that tote.

There were three envelopes left. One had Clarisse's name on it. It contained her birth and death certificates. The second had Morton's vital statistic pages. The third was written in a very shaky hand.

It was without a doubt Ring-a-ding's handwriting. It was not like her usual script though. Until the last few months of her life, her handwriting had still been clear and strong. This was more quivery and emotional. It was written with a ball point pen. She had actually torn through the paper in a place or two.

*"My dearest darling Charlie is dying. It is his wish that I write this letter for him. He wants to confess his sins before he dies, he says. I am to write what he tells me. I am to say at the very beginning that I didn't know anything about any of this.*

*I am an old man and I will be dead soon. I tried to be a good man, but I have sinned. I have taken the life of a living person. I did it willfully and knowing exactly what I was doing.*

*I never told anyone but the Lord what I had done. I have asked for his forgiveness many times. I hope he has granted it to me. I want to see my Belle in Heaven. If Jesus doesn't forgive me, I will go to Hell and never see her again.*

*Belle doesn't know anything about this. I never told her. You cannot hold her accountable for anything. This is a terrible burden I am putting on her now.*

*We had two beautiful children. But Morton was beautiful only on the outside. He was a charmer, but he was like a snake. He could charm you to your face, and then bite you when you turned your back.*

*I didn't know he was running moonshine. I knew he ran around with the Purvis boys, and their paw made white lightening. I knew Morton was drinking. I didn't know he had a car and was delivering liquor for Orville Purvis. I never did condone drinking. I saw too many men make fools of themselves under the influence of drink. Alcohol and farm work don't mix. Farming is a dangerous business. Alcohol makes you careless.*

*I had hoped that Morton would settle down. Belle wanted him to get married. She thought that would help. Morton would have this farm of ours. There was a parcel on the northeast side that I had saved for him to build a house for his family. It's a flat, pretty piece of land.*

*I had set aside a nice piece of dirt for Clarisse, too. She loved walking around the stream that fed the pond. Her piece has a stream with a little waterfall on it. She liked to play in that little waterfall. She'd sail leaves down the creek.*

*Our farm is in the front. Their dirt is half as wide as this place. Both have 70 acres. With our farm there'd be 425 acres. Our place would be split down the middle and each would get half when we were gone.*

*But that didn't happen. When both our children died early, Belle and I decided to leave everything to her niece, Grace, and her husband, James. They took care of us as good as our own children would have. Then they had Patty. She became Belle's and my baby. Belle used to sew and embroider a lot. Baby always had pretty clothes. She stayed with us as much as she could.*

*I taught her how to shoot. She can ride a cow as well as a horse. She loved that old plow horse, Dan. Baby lived with us after her mama and daddy were killed in that logging accident. She went away to college to be a teacher. Her mama and daddy left her in good shape with money, but all she had to do was ask, and I'd have given Baby everything I had.*

*But this is about my confession of my sin. I know Belle is writing and crying. I am rambling around with my story. These days I find it hard to stay on track. I am spending more and more of my time in the past.*

*Morton was mean. He came into this world mean. He would throw temper tantrums and hit me and Belle. He said cruel things. He was hateful to us and to Clarisse. He could go to town and be a charmer, but his true self was mean as a stripped snake and just as venomous.*

*When he was drinking, he'd come home cussing and throwing things around. Morton was strong. He was short, but muscular. I've seen him pick up the back end of a loaded wagon to get the wheel off the ground. Belle and I were both scared of him when he was drunk. We'd lock our door and take Clarisse into our bed.*

*Then one day, Belle took me into the front parlor. "Charlie, we got a problem with Morton." I knew Morton was trouble, but Belle was white as a sheet. She had been crying.*

*We sat down in front of the fireplace. She took my hands. "Clarisse got in the bed with us last night. Remember?"*

*Of course, I did. Clarisse had started having bad dreams. I'd wake up in the morning, and she'd be curled up with her doll and quilt at the bottom of the bed. She wouldn't tell us what the dreams were about, but she was having them off and on.*

*"It isn't a dream, Charlie. I wish it was, but it isn't. Clarisse told me this morning. I was helping her change her night dress. There was a little blood stain on her dress. She pulled it down over her knees and said 'Don't.' Then she went to crying.*

*I put her in my lap and ask her what the matter was. She was crying so hard. She kept pointing to herself and saying Morton. Morton has been molesting Clarisse at night. I put her to bed in our room. I went to Morton's room, but he was already gone. Did you know he is locking his door? The spare key is gone, too. I wonder what else he is hiding."*

*Belle had calmed down while she was telling me all this. I wanted to scream and yell and beat my boy half to death. If he'd been in the room, I might just have done that.*

*I went to Clarisse then. She was playing with her doll. I sat down and asked her if Morton was bothering her at night. She wouldn't look at me, but she did nod her little head. I asked if he bothered her during the day, and she shook her head no. Belle was sitting next to her on the bed. "Show your daddy what you showed me." That baby girl started poking her finger between the doll's legs.*

*I told her "It won't happen again, my sweet baby girl. I picked her up and took her downstairs."*

*Belle fixed her something to eat while I called Doc Morgan. I told him on the phone what had happened. He told me to let her play in warm water as long as she wanted. That would help with the tenderness. "What are you going to do, Charlie?"*

*I told him I was going to make Morton leave this house. He'd never be allowed near Clarisse again. Doc said he would stop by the house that evening. He'd come before Clarisse went to bed. He'd check on her.*

*Doc did come that night, but it wasn't for what we had planned.*

*Morton was over at the Purvis farm. He was pretty liquored up. He had been seeing a married woman. Her husband had found out. What I heard was that there were words between them. They kept jawing at each other and kept drinking. I was told that Morton and the other man got into a fist fight. His name was Tom Black. Morton always had a gun and a knife on him. Morton got shoved onto the blades of a circular tiller. He fired one shot and hit Tom Black in the stomach.*

*A couple of his liquored-up buddies brought Morton home in the back of a pickup truck. They carried him upstairs and dumped him in the bed. They said he'd shot a man. Morton was bad hurt, too. Then they just left in their truck.*

*I called Doc Morgan. He was already at the other man's house. Mrs. Morgan said he'd be at our place as soon as he could get there. Belle was putting pressure on the back of Morton's head. She told me he had some bad cuts on his back, too.*

*Doc got there about an hour or so later. By that time, the sheriff and others had heard about it. They had come to our house. A couple of women went upstairs to help Belle with Morton. Clarisse came downstairs frightened and crying. I picked her up and held her in my arms.*

*I told them I needed to be upstairs. Sheriff Bradley was a good man.*

*"You go, Charlie. Let me have this little princess. Bradley's wife was there with their youngest girl. She and Clarisse played together. Betty, Bradley, and their daughter took Clarisse to their car. Bradley put Clarisse in the back seat with his little girl. Betty climbed in the back with them. Sometime that night, Betty took both girls home and put them to bed.*

*The sheriff told me what he could about what happened. "I'll know more tomorrow when ol' man Purvis and those boys are sobered up."*

*Doc came down the steps. He asked me to go into one of the other rooms with him. "It's bad, Charlie. Belle is there with him, so I didn't tell her yet. Morton has some deep cuts on his back. I stitched them up and covered them with bandages. The biggest problem we have now is that Morton hit his head. I think he must have hit on one the disks. It is a deep cut. I'm sure his skull has a fracture in it. I can't tell how bad it is. I don't know if he'll live, but if he does, he won't ever be right again. I am afraid to move him to the hospital tonight. He is in really bad shape."*

*Morton never regained consciousness. He would open his eyes and lift his hand. He didn't respond to anything we said. I don't think he even knew we were in the room or touching him.*

*A couple of his drinking buddies came by. We let them see him. They all seemed to think Morton was going to be okay. Between them and the sheriff, we pretty well learned what happened. Tom Black, the man Morton shot, died the next morning. Doc said he couldn't live long. It was a gut shot.*

*Clarisse came home the next morning. Belle asked if she wanted to see Morton, but she shook her head no. Belle didn't think we should make her. I didn't either. She never saw Morton alive again. Her last contact with him was the night he put his hands on her.*

*Morton had made it to the fourth morning after being hurt. He was worse. I was alone with him in his room. I looked at my handsome son. So still in the bed. Such an evil heart in such a beautiful casing. I thought about my sweet little Clarisse and what she had been through at his hands.*

*Clarisse was staying with Belle's sister's family. She had her cousins to play with. We knew Louisa and Eli would tend to her until we could bring her back home.*

*Belle was downstairs. Some ladies had brought food over. They were sitting in the front parlor. Belle hadn't left Morton's side. She was tired. I made her go down to visit with her friends. She needed a few minutes out of the sick room.*

*It was wrong. I know it was wrong. The pillow was lying there next to his head. I picked it up. I put it over his face. I just stood there pressing down. He didn't resist. He sort of lifted his right hand like he had been doing. Then it just fell back on the bed. I just stood there, pressing down.*

*I don't know how long it was. I heard Doc on the steps coming up. I took the pillow and laid it back on the bed. I knew my son was dead. Dead by my hands. His father's hands.*

*"Charlie, how's our boy this morning. Any change?" asked Doc.*

*"Yes" I said. "Morton is dead. I have just been sitting with him." I remember a tear slid down my cheek.*

*"I'm sorry, Charlie. Does Belle know?"*

*I just shook my head.*

*Doc made me leave the room while he did an examination. "Charlie, I know this is hard to take, but this is a blessing. Morton probably would have spent the rest of his life without knowing anything. He'd have been a vegetable. This was the right thing to have happened."*

*"Let me get Belle. You sit back down."*

*I didn't know if Doc knew what had happened or not. He went to the parlor. I heard him call Belle. The other ladies got real quiet. Doc had made the bed up and pulled the covers up to Morton's chin. He looked like the sleeping little boy I had loved. I noticed the pillow I had used was in a chair. The pillowcase was gone. Doc knew. I am sure he knew. He never* told anybody, but he knew I had killed my own child that afternoon.

Belle sat with Morton and patted his hand. Then Doc pulled the sheet up over Morton's face. He led us downstairs. He went in the front parlor. He told the visitors that Morton had passed away. The pastor's wife stood and led everyone in a prayer for Morton's soul. I hoped someone would pray for mine.

Doc called the sheriff and the undertaker. They arrived at almost the same time. Belle went upstairs and got Morton's best suit, shirt, and tie. Sheriff Bradley took the clothes from her and walked her back downstairs. I heard Sheriff Bradley ask Doc Morton if there was anything he needed to know.

"No, Morton died of his injuries. I will fill out the death certificate when I get back to the office. They can go ahead and prep him for burial. I am going to stay here for a little bit longer. Charlie looks like he is about to faint. He was with him at the last."

After they carried Morton's body from his room, I shut the door. I have never been in that room again. That shut door reminds me every day of my life that I killed him. I have grieved over him before he died, and I have grieved over him since he died.

We buried Morton two days later.

Clarisse seemed to be doing well with Morton gone. I realized that Belle and I weren't so nervous anymore. We'd been so scared of our own child.

Clarisse got scarlet fever and then the pneumonia. When she died, I thought Belle would die, too. We'd lost both our children.

Please forgive me, Belle. I still think I did the right thing for Morton, for Clarisse, and for us. Dear Jesus, take me in your arms and offer me your forgiveness."

Uncle Charlie's shaky signature was there. Belle's was right under it.

I lay my head down on the table and sobbed.

# Chapter 89

"William. William. Honey. Wake up." I jostled him until Ramona got aggravated and jumped down.

William opened his eyes. "Wow. I went to sleep. Are you okay? Have you been crying?"

"Yes, you did. You sawed a good pile of lumber with those snores of yours." I tried to laugh. "But William, I need you to see something. Come in the kitchen."

"The picture was a peacock. Clarisse had drawn it. I found another one in an envelope from the safety deposit box. If I had any sense left, I would have realized it, but I didn't. It didn't even cross my mind when I pulled out my peacock tote bag. I think she was trying to tell me to look in my bag. I want you to read this letter from Uncle Charlie."

I went to the bathroom. I washed my face again while he read. My eyes were still red and puffy.

He was sitting at the table staring off in space. "That answers some questions, doesn't it? I don't think you should ever share this letter with anyone else. If anything, destroy it. Your Uncle Charlie and Aunt Belle suffered for years with this."

"I have been thinking about it. I want to go over to the house tonight. I want to talk to Morton and Clarisse. Will you come with me? I am going to confront Morton with this letter."

"Sure, I'll take you. What do you think this will accomplish though?" William stood up from the table.

"I don't think it will do anything, but it will help me. I always felt uneasy in Morton's room. Now I know why. He was an evil man, and now he is an evil spirit. I am going to tell him so tonight. I am just mad at him for being such an awful person that his own daddy had to take such action. My Uncle Charlie was a kind man. Can you imagine what this did to him?"

Everyone was gone from the house when we got there. The kitchen light was on. We had been leaving it on at night. As we entered from the porch, I flipped on the light in the front room.

We went on upstairs. All the doors were open, except Morton's. It seemed Morton was able to close the door, no matter what we used to prop it open.

I went in. There was that familiar smell of decay. It wasn't strong. It was just there. "Morton, are you in here? Would you come in your room if you are not here already? I want to talk to you. Actually, I want to read you something."

The door slammed shut behind me. "Patty, the door locked. Open it up. Please. Patty, unlock this door."

"I'm okay, William. Wait for me just outside the door. I think Morton and I are going to have a very important visit."

"Morton, I know what happened. Your daddy dictated a letter to your mama while he was dying. Belle didn't know anything about what your daddy did. I am going to read this letter to you. I want you to know what it says. Are you ready?"

The smell began to intensify just a little. I opened the letter and began to read. The smell kept getting stronger. When I got to the part about Clarisse, the papers were jerked from my hand. "I know what it says. I can read it, or I can tell you what a bastard you were to that child and to your parents. Get over yourself, Morton. You put them all through hell for your entire life. Now listen." I gathered up the papers and began reading again.

"Patty, are you okay? It stinks awfully bad around this door."

"I'm okay. Morton's not though. He is pitching a little fit to make me stop. I am not going to stop, Morton. Behave yourself and listen."

The entire room was filled with that mist I had seen earlier. The stench was becoming over- powering. "Pitch one, Morton. Pitch a good one. This is the last time you try scare me or anybody else. I am not afraid you anymore, you Stinking Little Fog. Show me your worse."

Perhaps I should not have told him that last part. He decided he would show out then. The pages were again jerked out of my hands. The fog was more intense. Oh, so was the smell. I was determined I would not gag and give this jerk any pleasure in my discomfort.

"Listen to me, Morton. You are done. Blow smoke; stink up the place. I don't care. We know just how terrible you were. We know what happened to you. Your story is out. I am sorry that Uncle Charlie had to kill you. I really am. But I am sorrier you were the kind of person you were. You died not because Charlie smothered you but because you were such an evil being. They were afraid of you. You were so violent and hateful that your own parents feared you. Morton, you were a bully. A selfish bully. You were a child molester, and a drunk, and no telling what else.

"I think your daddy did the bravest thing in the world when he smothered you. You would not have been a normal person again. Oh wait, you weren't normal to start with, were you? Now open that damn door. You can sit in here and rot for all I care."

I pulled the door open and stepped into William's arms.

## Chapter 90

"I need to go outside for a minute, William."

We went out on the front porch. I breathed in some clean air. My head was throbbing, and I was nauseated from the stench.

"I could hear you through the door. I couldn't budge it though. There was vapor coming up from the floor and around the door jam. You had me scared to death. I was about to get that electric saw and cut my way in when you opened the door." William continued to hold my shaking hands.

"I'm okay, now, Honey. I have a headache, but it isn't bad—not like the other night. I'd like to know if the mist is still up there, but I don't want to go check. I am pretty sure he is going to retaliate against me. Will you take me home and stay? I don't want to be by myself right now."

On the way home in the car, it all hit me. I started shaking and crying. William pulled into the drug store parking lot. We sat there for about ten minutes holding hands. We talked about it all again. "You are the bravest woman--no, person, I know. You were great." He kissed me on the forehead. He held me for a few more minutes. I finally stopped crying. We went back to my house.

I pulled my clothes off as I entered the kitchen door. I smelled like Morton. I might just burn them instead of washing them.

"Drink this and take these aspirin." William handed me a glass of water.

I got in the shower. I felt a lot better when I got out. I joined William on the sofa and curled up next to him. Ramona was in his lap, and Randolph was curled against my legs. I went fast asleep. I guess I was wiped out after the adrenaline rush of confronting Morton.

The next morning, the cats and I were on the sofa. William was gone. "I left about 5:00. I couldn't' wake you. I figured you needed that deep sleep after everything that happened. Call me when you get up. I work this morning, but I will come if you need me. I get off at 3:00 today. I love you, my brave girl."

My head was so clear. I felt re-energized. Maybe I needed to throw a temper tantrum more often myself.

I called William. I told him I felt great. Relieved. I planned to do some packing at my house today. He would come by after work. The cats and I had breakfast. I changed into shorts and a t-shirt to tackle my closets. I called Sheila, the consignment lady, and asked if I could bring some things by tomorrow. She said I could.

I pulled out clothes I hadn't worn in a long time. Each time I laid something on the bed Ramona jumped on top of it. "You do realize that not everyone wants cat hair trim on their clothes, Young Lady?" I believe I heard Randolph snicker.

After the closet, I set to work on all the drawers. Once those were done. I tidily folded everything and placed them in boxes. I moved on to sweaters. I had a pile of clothes that was incredibly high. I called Sheila again.

"Would you mind if I bought some stuff over this afternoon?" I sounded a little pitiful, I thought.

"No, come ahead. I don't have any drop-offs today or tomorrow. I can get a head start on your things this afternoon."

"Dang, Patricia, did you empty out Belk's? I'm glad you brought these over today, so I can get started." Sheila pulled a rolling dress cart out and started hanging things on it. "Go get that rolling flat cart. We can put these bags and boxes on it."

Once unloaded and in the building, Sheila asked me "Are these Miss Belle's things?"

I explained I had given most of her house dresses to Dana for the fiber sculptures and the dolls she makes. What I had brought were mostly my things I either couldn't wear or wouldn't wear anymore.

I stopped at the Piggly Wiggly for chicken salad, strawberries, and romaine lettuce. We could have that for supper tonight. I wanted to go back to Belle's place. First, I wanted to go to the cemetery.

William came in a little after 3:00. "Have you had anything to eat? Want something?" I asked.

"No, I had a big lunch today. Miss Rachel sent to me to work with fried chicken, potato salad, and a peach pie. I am not sure I can marry you now. I have this really good thing going with my landlady."

After a few hugs and a few kisses, maybe a few more kisses and a cuddle or two, and well… about an hour later, I told him I wanted to go to the cemetery and over to Belle's.

I gathered up three big black trash bags. I needed to remove all the old flowers and clean the grave site. There were a couple of pretty artificial arrangements that had been sent to the funeral. I would put those about and clean the plot of all its wilted flowers. William grabbed a rake and put it in the back of his SUV.

# CHAPTER 91

The fresh flowers had needed to be thrown away. Nothing lasts long in this heat. I had left them here far too long. William pulled the flowers from the stands and out of the containers. I started putting the greenery in the plastic bags. We stacked all the pots and the stands together in the back of his car.

After everything was cleaned, I looked at William. "Please don't think I am crazy."

"Honey, I know you're crazy, but you seem only to be dangerous to yourself. What is it?"

"I want to talk to Ring-a-ding and Uncle Charlie."

"Go ahead. I'll load the car. I'll wander around. Call me when you want me." William walked toward the car with the bags.

I put one of the silk flower arrangements at Mama and Daddy's grave. I told them how much I missed them and how I still needed their guidance. There was a small basket of silk flowers I anchored next to Clarisse's head stone. I took another large floral arrangement and placed it between Charlie and Belle. Belle's death date had not been engraved on the tombstone yet. I needed to be sure enough gravel was in grave site. I thought I would get the stone company to re-gravel the entire plot.

"Ring-a-ding and Uncle Charlie, I met Morton and Clarisse. They are still at the house. Why aren't you there? I miss you both so much.

I found the letter. I understand why you did it, Uncle Charlie. You did the right thing. If my forgiving you helps in anyway, you know I give it freely. I know it was hard. It was the right thing for you to do. I can't believe how you kept that secret.

I've opened Morton's room. He is still there. He lets his presence be known by a terrible smell. Sometimes, he makes a foggy like mist. I read him your letter. He got really mad when I got the part about Clarisse. Maybe he didn't think anyone knew about it. He got angry a couple of other times, too. I told him I wasn't afraid of him. He could stay and stink up the place for all I cared.

Clarisse has come to me at night a few times. She gets in the bed with me. She may think I am you, Aunt Belle. I'm pretty sure Ramona and Randolph know she is there. They don't seem to be bothered by her. They don't like to go in Morton's space though. Me, either. I am going back by there tonight to check on everything. Mr. Horace and his crew are putting a bathroom in part of Morton's room. He may not like it, but he'll get used to it.

William and I are getting married December 13. I wish you were both here. I am wearing the ring you gave William when you gave him your blessings. Uncle Charlie, I have your wedding ring on my left thumb next to Daddy's. Ring-a-ding, your little wedding band is on my right little finger, next to Mama's. You are always with me. Always.

I think the house will be done in about another four or five weeks. Y'all bring Mama and Daddy and come see it. You know you are welcome. You can move in upstairs in your old room if you want. It's ready when you are. All of you are welcome to live with us."

I brushed tears from my eyes. I walked to where William was standing.

"You okay, Honey?"

"This is the best I've felt since Ring-a-ding died. I told them we were getting married. I invited them to over into the house. I told them about Clarisse and Morton and how he acted when I read the letter. I hope they are at peace, William."

"You did the right thing in telling them. You were right to tell Morton off last night. What do you want to do with this stuff from the cemetery?" he asked.

"I'll put the live stuff in the trash. I wish I had a compost pile. I guess I have enough stuff here to start one, don't I? Let's pour it out behind the old outhouse where Ring-a-ding once had a small composter bin. Stop at Edna's Flowers Galore. I am going to give her all these wire wreath stands. I don't know if she wants the plastic pots or not. If she doesn't, we'll donate them. Okay with you?"

We left everything at Edna's Flowers Galore. Miss Edna had a compost heap and wanted our stuff. She took all the pots. "I wash these in a bleach solution, and I use them to store new flowers coming in. You can never have too many backup pots. I try to keep fresh flowers at the nursing home and in my mama's room there. I really appreciate the wreath stands. Most people just throw them in the land fill. They are good to use again. They are great to stake up your tomatoes, too. When you get your garden going, come back, and I'll give you all you want."

# Chapter 92

We went upstairs. The bathroom wall was up. All the plumbing had been stubbed in. The shower stall had been set in place, too. It was exciting to see things moving along like this. We walked into Morton's room. Not a smell. Nothing.

I showed William what Mr. Horace had suggested about the closet and the two long rods. He liked the idea of drawers instead of open shelves under the window. "Drawers seem to contain clutter better than shelves."

We went into the other rooms. Clarisse's baby doll was still covered up. She had not used her pad or crayons. I left everything there just in case.

I think a bird flew into the windowpane in Morton's room. It sounded like that. We went back in. "You in here, Morton? Was that a bird, or did you make a thump? Are you still mad at me? I don't really care if you are. I saw your parents today. I told them about finding the letter. I told them how you acted, too. If you want to stay, I know I can't get rid of you. But you need to behave like the gentleman you were raised to be."

"Honey, stop. Look." William was pointed to a spot which used to be the center of the room. The smell was back.

"Hey, Morton. What do you want?" I asked in a bored voice.

The mist was back. The smell was even stronger now. The mist pulled itself together. It was not like the funnel shape that had formed and then melted into the bed. It was more column like. I wouldn't say it was shaped like a man, but more like that shape I saw attacking the bed. Slowly this arm like structure pulled out to the side of the column. It moved from side to side, parallel to the floor.

"Morton, I don't understand what you are telling me. Can you tell me any other way? Can you write on a paper?"

Still moving its arm from side to side, the column condensed. The arm slid back into the mist. The vapor rose toward the ceiling. There was clear space at the bottom as the fog thinned out. The whole thing glided upward. Then it vanished. So did the smell. There was no more odor lingering in the room. The air smelled fresh.

"Do you think Morton left?" I asked William.

"I don't know. I think that was a peaceful gesture to you. We'll only know if he stinks up the joint again."

# CHAPTER 93

I arrived at the house about 10:00 the next morning. Men were working upstairs and downstairs. Mr. Horace came down.

"Hey Patty, things are looking good upstairs. They got the shower in. The tile guy is up there now. You stay out of the upstairs bathroom, so the tiles will set. I'm glad you are using white tiles for both bathrooms' floors. Cleaner and easier to do with everything in one color."

"We'll get the toilet and sink done probably day after tomorrow. We want those tiles to be set and dry. Once the fixtures are in and functional, we'll get started on the downstairs bathroom."

"You just missed Casper. He came by to look at the two fireplaces where you want to put the mantels. He is like new man. He was even moving better. He had his cane, but he wasn't relying on it as much as he had been."

"I don't know what happened or what caused it, but the smell is gone. The guys didn't find any squirrels or birds dead in the attic. Whatever it was, it's gone now."

I smiled at him and told him it was the good job they had been doing. They must have run off an evil spirit. Secretly, I sent a thank you up to Heaven. I couldn't wait to call William with the news.

Mr. Horace and I shared coffee and a piece of Miss Rachel's carrot cake. Mr. Casper had left it on the table. Mr. Horace filled me in on the next things to happen. They were going to cut a door through to the downstairs bathroom from the porch side. The framer was going to start on the porch this afternoon. He gave me a list of things that required final decisions.

I called William when I got to the car. "Mr. Horace says the smell is completely gone upstairs."

"Halleluiah!!" William laughed. "That's great. I hope it never comes back."

I told him I was going to pick out colors for the walls. I needed to make a final decision on new kitchen cabinets and counter tops. William and I had discussed all the choices ad nauseum. We agreed to use white as much as possible in the kitchen.

William told me to get what I liked best. He was sure he'd be happy with everything. Lord, I hope he stayed this easy to live with when we got married.

# CHAPTER 94

Everything was progressing faster than expected. The bathrooms were beautiful. The sunroom was better than I could have hoped. Things fell into place with no problems.

Morton had not been back. I think Morton was freed when the story came out. He was trapped in anger and hatefulness. Knowing how Uncle Charlie and his mama had grieved told him he had been important to them. Morton would not have wanted to live trapped with a wounded brain. He was free.

Mr. Casper had done himself proud. Both mantels were gorgeous. He and Mr. Fordham set them in place. Mr. Fordham placed the gas logs and turned them on. "Now that there is a purdy sight, Patty. You'll be rocking your babies in front of that fireplace."

I had rehung most of the lace curtains. I brought new ones to replace those that were too tattered to use again. I had all the quilts cleaned. The colors were more vibrant than I could have hoped.

The kids had done a great job cleaning and polishing all the furniture. We did a good dusting. Each room sparkled in the daylight. Darryl replaced the old ceiling light fixtures with some vintage ones Keith had found.

The organ played again. I was practicing some on it. I was remembering a lot of the old songs Belle had taught me. Most of them were from the Cokesbury Hymnal.

I had Clarisse's dress and both of her peacock drawings framed. They hung in her room. Her patterned quilt was on the foot of her bed, with her baby doll and Bible. I left her room pretty much as it was. I visited with her every day. Her unused pad and crayons were on her bed.

We decided to make the downstairs bedroom next to the kitchen ours. That was where we first made love. It just seemed like the happiest place for us.

I had pulled boxes from storage that had been Mama and Daddy's things. The porcelain birds looked like they belonged where they were placed in the various rooms. I hung some of the pictures and placed others on dressers. The collection of vegetable china was on the kitchen stove along with some violets. I had grouped a few of the plants in the old cast iron skillets on the stove. They looked just right. Philodendron again trailed from the top of the antique stove.

The upstairs sewing room was an office space now. I had covered the old dressmaker's dummy in black velvet. Keith came over to go through the toolbox of jewelry. He coveted a lot of those things. We picked out some of the most beautiful pieces. He placed them on the dummy. He hung a long flapper like necklace of blue glass on the neck stump. Uncle Charlie's black dress hat sat on top of the neck. Then Keith went through the scarf trunk and pulled out a long black lace scarf and a black cut velvet one with lots of fringe.

"Hold this." Keith began to wrap the scarves, so they draped over the bottom of the dummy's hips. He angled one up, pushed the other down, and did a little twist. "Hand me those long pins." I did. "Give me that big opal and rhinestone job over there."

"Put your hand right there and don't move it." I did as instructed.

"Voila!" Keith threw up his hands in triumph.

He had created an angled skirt held in place with the big opal broach. Other jewels were scattered over the form. It was a work of art. Keith started taking pictures from every angle. "This is one of my masterpieces. It is going on my website as my centerpiece."

# CHAPTER 95

William and I got married. Pickle, William's mother, and sisters are the best of friends. They had the time of their lives plotting and planning. The wedding was beautiful.

William and I showed up and did what we were told.

William and his daddy wore black tuxedos. They were quite handsome. Pickle wore a cranberry red velvet dress that was tea length. She carried a bouquet of white roses with little red rose buds.

Miss Martha Kate worked her miracles. Ring-a-ding's dress was perfect. The lace that hung from the sleeves and bodice was so delicate and graceful. Instead of a veil, I wore a sweetheart hat. Cream colored straw in which the brim was set more upright at the back of my head so that my face wasn't covered. It was shaped like the top of a Valentine's heart. Miss Martha Kate had trimmed the brim with cranberry ribbon. Long streamers of the same fabric hung down past my shoulders. I wore the cranberry red sash. It had one of Belle's broaches with pearls and red stones pinned to it.

I carried a bouquet of cranberry red roses with white rose buds and baby's breath. Cranberry red ribbons cascaded down from the handle.

Clarisse left us a few weeks after the house was finished. She saw her room completed. I had put my teddy bear on Charlie's and Belle's bed downstairs. One day I went into Clarisse's room. My bear, her baby doll, and her little Bible were laying against the pillow on her bed.

Belle's place was now our place. It had a past, but now it also had a future.

The End.